i only
have pies
for you

Also by Suzanne Nelson

Cake Pop Crush

Macarons at Midnight

Hot Cocoa Hearts

You're Bacon Me Crazy

Donut Go Breaking My Heart

Sundae My Prince Will Come

i only have pies for you

Suzanne Nelson

SCHOLASTIC INC.

Copyright © 2019 by Suzanne Nelson

All rights reserved. Published by Scholastic Inc., *Publishers since 1920*. SCHOLASTIC and associated logos are trademarks and/or registered trademarks of Scholastic Inc.

The publisher does not have any control over and does not assume any responsibility for author or third-party websites or their content.

This book is a work of fiction. Names, characters, places, and incidents are either the product of the author's imagination or are used fictitiously, and any resemblance to actual persons, living or dead, business establishments, events, or locales is entirely coincidental.

ISBN 978-1-338-31641-4

10 9 8 7 6 5 4 3 2   19 20 21 22 23

Printed in the U.S.A. 40
First printing 2019

Book design by Jennifer Rinaldi

For the Lone Star State, and my alma
mater, Texas A&M University, where
I spent four deliciously life-changing years.
Texas, my heartstring is forever tied to yours.

—S.N.

Chapter One

I approached the oven with a mixture of hope and trepidation. Could it be that I'd *finally* done it? I reached for the handle, then hesitated, breathing deep. The pie definitely smelled right. The kitchen of Pies N' Prattle was steeped in the scents of caramelized butter, cinnamon, and apples. A promising sign.

I opened the oven a crack and peeked in. *No!* The caramel apple pie I'd spent my entire afternoon making looked like a natural disaster. The crust was a sinkhole, cratering into the caramel apple filling; only its sad, crinkled edges remained.

I ripped off my oven mitts and launched them across the room, letting out a cry of frustration. I'd always had a temper worse than a grease fire—flaring in an instant and tough to douse. My parents often laughed about the fervor with which I'd thrown myself on the floor as a toddler whenever I was told I had to eat my peas or go to bed. It wasn't a trait I was proud of, but I never could seem to get a handle on it, either. In fact, I might've hollered again over my pie fiasco if the muffled voices of our customers in the main room hadn't stopped me.

"*¿Qué pasó?*" I heard Mrs. Gonzalez say. "Is that Dacey? Is she all right?"

Mom's bell-like laughter sounded from the other side of the kitchen door. "She's fine. Just doing some baking is all. She's so much like her great-grandma Hazel . . . a bundle of pint-sized passion, especially when it comes to pies."

Like GG Hazel? I scoffed, staring at my sunken pie. I'd never known GG Hazel in person. She'd died long before I was born. I knew about her, though. Every person in Bonnet, Texas, did. There was one, universally acknowledged truth about Hazel Culpepper: That woman could bake pies.

And I couldn't. But Mom kept insisting on this resemblance I supposedly had to GG Hazel. As if Mom's saying it might give me the pie gene that seemed to have skipped my DNA.

"Dacey?" Mom stuck her head around the door. A quick scan of the kitchen told her I was alive and well, but she still said, "Scale of one to ten, hangnail to Armageddon. Go."

Mom had played this game with me for as long as I could remember, asking me to pick a number on a scale of one to ten as a way of gauging the severity of any problem. It was her not-so-subtle way of reminding me to control my temper.

"Two," I mumbled grudgingly. "Not Armageddon, but my pie *does* look like it's been hit by a meteor."

"Caramel apple *crumble* it is, then." Mom smiled. "You come from a long line of great pie bakers, Dace. Don't worry so much. You'll grow into your talent." She took my apple "crumble" out of the oven and slid it into a pastry box. I had no idea what poor victim Mom might give it to, but I hoped I'd never set eyes on the disaster again. "Now come on out and say hi to every-body. They've been asking after you."

I followed Mom through the swinging doors. The snug main room—painted a cheery daffodil yellow and crowded with armchairs, settees, and coffee tables—instantly brightened my mood. More than that, though, were the waves, smiles, and "hello"s I got from the dozen or so folks in the shop.

There was Mrs. Gonzalez with her fussy baby Marco and little daughter Alma. There was Mrs. Beaumont and her Friday afternoon knitting group. Mr. Jenkins and Mr. Walker were arguing over their game of Scrabble, and Ms. Jackson was working on the romance novel she'd been swearing she'd have finished by the summer solstice. They weren't customers so much as permanent fixtures in Pies N' Prattle. They'd been coming to our shop since before I was born, and knew almost as much about my life as Mom and Dad did.

It was like having a bunch of aunts, uncles, and grandparents watching over me 24/7—and not just in our shop, either. Our small, homespun town of Bonnet was bordered by the Brazos River on one side and the Jenkins cattle ranch on the other. A hiccup took longer than a drive down our main street. Bonnet's single traffic light had made the front page of the *Bonnet Times* when it had finally been installed two years ago, and Bonneters loved to boast about the bona fide hitching post that still stood, as it had for over a century, outside The Chicken Shack. But people looked after each other in Bonnet, and it gave the town a coziness and familiarity that I loved.

"Don't forget, Selena," Mom said to Mrs. Gonzalez, who was leaving with Alma and the squalling Marco in her arms. "Two slices of the lavender honey pie an hour before you nurse Marco and you'll both sleep through the night. You'll see."

Mrs. Gonzalez hugged her, gushing her thanks, then waved to me and headed out.

"Poor Selena," Mom murmured. "A colicky newborn and now her restaurant closing its doors next month."

Together, we stared out the window at The Whole Enchilada—the tiny but delicious Tex-Mex restaurant the Gonzalez family owned on Main Street. It sat between two vacant stores; those had once been the Bonnet Soda Shop and Shoe-La-La Consignment.

"That's the fifth business to close in the last six months," I said. "And we're not even counting the Longhorn Loop."

Just saying the name of Texas's oldest wooden roller coaster made my throat hitch. It wasn't that I was particularly attached to the ride. But when the coaster closed six months ago, the loss of the tourist attraction had been a virtual death knell for Bonnet's businesses. Visits from out-of-towners had always been few and far between. Still, for over a century, Bonnet had boasted two claims to fame: Hazel Culpepper's pie shop and the Longhorn Loop. Now we had only the pie shop left, and the tourists were dwindling.

"It's not good," Mom said. A second later, she straightened her shoulders, adding, "*But* it's no use drowning in a river of worry, either."

There it was. Mom's glass-half-full MO. She smiled at our shop full of regulars. "We have our tried-and-true Bonneters." Then she turned to the picture of GG Hazel that hung on the wall, alongside Hazel's favorite apron. The photo was part of a framed article from the *Bonnet Times*, May of 1945. Mom reached out and pressed her fingertips to Hazel's cheek. "And we have GG Hazel to inspire us. I just wish we still had her Heartstring Pie, too. Now *that* would be something folks would talk about all over Texas."

A reverent hush fell over the shop at Mom's mention of Heartstring Pie. There wasn't a soul in Bonnet who hadn't heard the stories about my great-grandmother's most famous pie and the supposed "curse" surrounding it. Nor was there a soul who hadn't, at one time or another, hoped to be the one to find the missing recipe for it.

"I had a piece of Heartstring Pie," a gravelly voice said behind us. It was Mr. Jenkins. With his six-foot-four-inch frame, thick silver mustache, and broad build, he might've seemed imposing, except that I'd known him my entire life. "Just once when I was eight." His expression softened into nostalgia. "Hazel brought me a slice after my mama's passing. I didn't want to touch a bite of it at first. Couldn't eat a thing, let alone talk or even cry. But Hazel, she leaned over me and said, 'Now, Jeb, just the tiniest nibble will ease you. It won't stop the hurting, but it'll make it tolerable.' She spoon-fed me a bite and, next thing I knew, I was in her lap, the floodgates open." He shook his head. "Strangest thing, too, but it *did* help. I don't know how, but it did."

I'd heard Mr. Jenkins's story many times before, and it always gave me a little tingle of warmth, like there was a part of me that believed there *was* some magic in that pie. But then I brushed the thought away. I knew it was a silly idea.

"That sounds like Hazel's Heartstring Pie, for sure," Mom said reverently. GG Hazel had passed away when Mom was only five. Even though Mom didn't remember her, she'd grown up steeped in Hazel's larger-than-life legend, fostering a loyalty so deep that she felt "called," as she put it, to do right by Hazel and the pie shop. "That pie was a treasure."

"Miss Edie?" Mr. Jenkins said to Mom. "Speaking of pie, could I get a slice of your pecan pie for my Mazie? Her rheumatism's acting up again and we've got company coming—"

"Of course." Mom flew behind the sales counter to box up the pie. "And I'm sending you home with a slice of pineapple pie, too. Just the trick for aching bones." Mr. Jenkins reached for his wallet, but Mom waved it away. "On the house."

Mr. Jenkins clucked his tongue. "Edie, how many times have I told you to quit giving your pies away for free?"

Mom put her hands on her hips, feigning indignation. "Jeb, you run your ranch the way you see fit, and I'll do the same for my shop."

He gave a deep chuckle, tipped his Stetson cattleman hat to her, then smiled at me as he headed for the door. "Dacey, I'll see you at the stables in the morning?"

I felt a swell of excitement. I boarded my horse, Ginger, at the Jenkins ranch and I never missed a day of riding if I could help it. "Count on it!" I told him.

I'd been riding Ginger in Western horse shows since I'd gotten her in the third grade, and I'd taken riding lessons at the ranch long before that. Dad teased that if he hadn't witnessed the event himself, he would've sworn I was born in a saddle. My temper never got the better of me when I was around horses. I itched to be riding Ginger now—instead of stuck here at the pie shop.

I could feel GG Hazel's gaze on me, as if she'd heard my thoughts. I studied the black-and-white photograph, taking in Hazel's fair skin, wavy black bob, small mouth, slightly crooked nose, wide-set eyes, and dark arched brows.

Mom didn't much resemble Hazel, but everyone was always commenting that I did. I couldn't see it. Yes, I had Hazel's dark hair, though mine was longer, curlier, and more unruly, usually tied back in a mussed knot. But her eyes were nothing like mine. Hers had a confident clarity and an almost clairvoyant quality that made people believe she could help them with whatever troubles they brought before her. Of course, that glimmer in her expression might also have been pride in the flawless Heartstring Pie she offered up to the camera.

What I apparently *had* inherited from her was her temper. The story went that Hazel had once pitched an entire banana cream pie at Bonnet's mayor, simply because he'd suggested removing Main Street's old hitching post. How bad did my luck have to be that I'd gotten GG Hazel's only flaw and none of her charms?

I sighed and scanned the newspaper article for the hundredth time.

HAZEL CULPEPPER BAKES UP HEALING AND HOPE

Just days after D-Day, our own Hazel Culpepper, alongside other Red Cross volunteers, was saving the lives and lifting the spirits of dozens of American soldiers at Normandy Beach, France. Only it isn't her nursing skill that's earned her the nickname "Healing Hazel"; it's her pie. Since returning to Bonnet, Hazel's been busy baking up pies for our returning veterans.

"I saw our boys suffering," she says. "Many were weary and shell-shocked. Some were plain brokenhearted from what they'd seen and done. The best comfort I could offer was a lending ear to hear their sorrows, and a pie to please their bellies."

Hazel and her Heartstring Pie, in particular, are earning the admiration and devotion of every veteran for miles around.

"Hazel has a knack for knowing when a soldier's down," Fred Cooper says. "That's when she comes knocking with her Heartstring Pie. One slice, and peace settles in my soul. I can't ever forget the war, but I do take some comfort from Hazel and her pie."

The article, I knew, had been reprinted in papers from Houston to Dallas, and soon much of Texas was flooding in to visit Bonnet for a taste of the famous Heartstring Pie.

Only now, the Heartstring Pie recipe was gone, and the pie with it. According to Mom, GG Hazel had hidden the recipe years ago, when she discovered that my grandma Mabel planned to turn the pie into a moneymaking machine. Mabel began claiming the pie could work legit miracles, from curing cancer to preventing aging, and she was going to sell the recipe for a pretty penny to anyone desperate enough to believe.

"Hazel never wanted the recipe to be misused like that," Mom had told me. "She didn't want anyone selling Heartstring Pie for a profit and cheating folks into believing the pie was some sort of eternal life elixir."

After GG Hazel died, Grandma Mabel never gave up

searching for that recipe, even when she retired and passed the pie shop along to Mom. No one in Bonnet knew where Hazel had hidden the recipe. But lots of people tried to re-create the pie without knowing *what* had gone into it. And the strange thing? Each attempt someone made ended in disaster.

Stories abounded of Heartstring knockoffs that smelled like skunk or putrid socks. One pie simply exploded, without any explanation, covering half the congregation of the Bonnet Baptist church in a purple stain that took weeks to wash off. Worst of all was the pie that Grandma Mabel made, which, when she sliced into it, produced a poor little mouse. Mabel never understood how that mouse got into the pie, and Mom swore she was still muttering about it with her very last breath.

Was it a true curse? I didn't believe in that sort of nonsense. But that didn't stop Bonnet folks from being superstitious about the Heartstring Pie, and lifting it onto a pedestal of magic. No one could duplicate that pie, and nothing else could ever compare to it in deliciousness or mysterious healing properties.

"I believe that recipe's still hidden somewhere," Mom liked to say with a smile. "Tucked into a cozy nook, waiting for the right Culpepper to discover it."

I always rolled my eyes at this, but I wondered about the whereabouts of that recipe, too. Sometimes I almost felt tempted to look for it, but then caught myself. If GG Hazel's spirit did still linger, she'd make sure that her recipe *never* fell into the hands of a failure of a pie baker like me.

Besides, the recipe had probably been destroyed decades ago, disintegrating in our Texas humidity in whatever ancient hole GG Hazel had stuck it in.

"Did Hazel finally give up the secret today?" a voice behind me said teasingly.

I whirled around to see my best friend, Zari, grinning at me. Her big eyes—the color of blackberries—glimmered from her heart-shaped face.

On the outside, Zari and I were opposites; while my hair was long and messy, hers was cropped short and cute. My skin was pale and freckled; hers was dark brown. I was tall; she was petite. But we'd been attached at the hip practically since birth.

"What a headline that would make," Zari continued, peering at Hazel's photo, "'Famous Heartstring Pie Recipe Rediscovered At Last!'"

"Zari!" I laughed, exasperated. "It's never going to happen. And would you please quit sneaking up on me like that?" The girl had a talent for slinking in and out of rooms.

"How else do you expect me to get decent scoops?" She shrugged, then snagged the slice of Lemon Zinger pie waiting for her on the sales counter. Zari stopped by the shop almost every day after school, and Mom always had a piece of her favorite pie waiting.

We sat down together at a table and Zari dug into her slice. "A skilled investigative journalist has to keep her eyes and ears open to everything," my best friend went on. "It's how Pulitzers are won and the best news written."

"News?" I raised an eyebrow. Zari wrote a weekly "Buzz" column for *The Beehive*, the Bonnet Middle School paper, but whether its content qualified as news was debatable.

I ducked as she launched a napkin at my head.

"Hey!" Zari cried. "It's not my fault our fishbowl of a town isn't at the forefront of current affairs. But I report the truth. And if the truth is that Ms. Aberdine has fifty cats living in her basement, or that Mr. Victor's pig got loose and ate every geranium in Mrs. Beaumont's window boxes—"

"That pig did indeed!" Mrs. Beaumont interjected, looking up from her knitting. "Mark my words, that Tootsie will get her comeuppance someday . . ."

"Then," persisted Zari, ignoring Mrs. Beaumont's interruption, "it's my duty to share it. The last decent story I had was when Mrs. Crenshaw declared she'd discovered the Heartstring Pie recipe buried in a sarsaparilla bottle under her front porch."

"That *was* a doozy!" Ms. Jackson whistled, pausing over her typewriter. "That pie she baked gave her entire family hives for weeks!"

"*The curse,*" Mrs. Beaumont murmured with a shake of her head.

That brought a round of knowing chuckles from everyone in

the room except for me and Zari. We exchanged an amused glance; we didn't believe in the "curse."

Zari slapped her messenger bag onto the table, jabbing a finger at the design printed on its label: a replica of a New York City street grid. "Right here. Forty-First and Eighth Avenue. That's where my destiny lies."

"The *New York Times*." I grinned at her. "I know. You're going to be the chief current affairs correspondent."

"I hope so. My soul is a New Yorker's. But"—Zari paused for dramatic effect—"I *do* have a real piece of news today. Something way bigger than cats and pigs. Only, I'm not sure how you're going to take it." She looked at me with conflicting flickers of excitement and hesitation.

My muscles clenched. I'd never seen Zari worried about spilling news before. "If this is about another store closing, I don't want to know."

Zari shook her head. "Just promise not to freak out, okay?"

I nodded impatiently.

She took a deep breath, then let the words fly in a furious tumble. "ChaytonFreedellisbackintown."

I blinked. My heart tripped. "I didn't hear you right. Chayton Freedell is . . . back?" I hadn't said that name in two years, and it tasted bitter on my tongue.

"He is," Zari squeaked.

"What?" I shrieked, and Mrs. Beaumont dropped her knitting to clutch her chest.

"Everything's fine," Zari reassured everyone, then lowered her voice at me. "Breathe. I know you said you never wanted to see him again, but don't go Hulk on me."

I pressed my palms into the table. "Don't you remember what he *did* to me?" I hissed.

"The parade disaster?" Zari scoffed. "Of course I do. I was the one who spent hours helping you wash the pie out of your hair."

I shuddered at the memory. When I was ten, Chayton Freedell and I had ridden our horses side by side in the Bonnet County Fair parade. Only Chayton started fooling around, like he always did, snagging people's hats off their heads, lying across the back of his horse and pretending to slide off. I told him to quit, but did he listen? Nooooooo. Course not. Instead, he spooked my Ginger until she bucked me off. I flew through the air and crashed into the Pies N' Prattle booth, right atop the fifty huckleberry pies stacked sky-high for the fair's pie-eating contest.

"He *did* apologize," Zari reminded me gently.

"It wasn't a real apology!" I remembered the tightness in Chayton's voice, like he was trying to keep from busting up laughing, which he'd been doing only a minute before, along with most of the population of Bonnet.

"Dacey, it was two years ago. You've changed a lot since then. He probably has, too."

"Not enough." It wasn't just about the pie fiasco; it was everything else that had led up to it, too. Chayton sat next to me in every class from kindergarten on, whispering knock-knock jokes and drawing cartoons he thrust in my face, whether I asked to see them or not. We were neck and neck for our grades in every subject. Somehow, he always ended up doing book reports on the same book as me, studying the same battle for every social studies project, and even tying me for second place in the spelling bee. The epic horse/pie disaster had been the last straw. When he'd moved away, I told myself I'd never have to speak to him again.

I dropped my head to the table, my anger fizzling into dismay. "Why is he back?" I groaned.

"Um, did you forget his grandpa lives here?"

"No," I said grudgingly. I just didn't like to think about the fact that Mr. Jenkins was related to Chayton at all.

"And you like Mr. Jenkins."

"Because Mr. Jenkins isn't anything like Chayton!" I looked up at Zari and frowned. "Irritating, show-off, know-it-all—"

"Generosity of spirit, Dace," Mom interjected, coming over. "What's this about now?"

"Good news for Bonnet, actually, Miss Edie," Zari chirped. "Do you remember Julip Freedell?" Mom nodded, and I resisted the urge to roll my eyes. Chayton's mom was now famous as the host of the über-popular cooking and lifestyle show *Prairie*

Living. Julip traveled all over Texas scouting for obscure craft ideas, antiques, and recipes.

"I just saw Mrs. Freedell at the middle school," Zari explained. "She was registering Chayton for classes. She's come back to Bonnet to film a special 'Homecoming' episode of her show. It's going to feature the Bonnet County Fair and pie-eating contest!"

"Well." If it were possible for Mom to look even cheerier than usual (which was a tall order, believe me), she did. "I'd call that news better than good. Julip's show might breathe some life back into Bonnet, and bring in some fresh customers."

"*And* save us from boredom," Zari put in. "Newcomers mean intrigue and scandals and—"

"Trouble," I grumbled.

Zari shook her head at me. "It'll be fine. You'll hardly notice Chayton's back at all."

All I could picture was my ten-year-old self, covered head to toe in huckleberry pie. I cringed. Hardly notice the return of my archnemesis? Not a chance.

Chapter Two

The next morning, I reached the Jenkins ranch as the sun rose. First light streamed through the windows of the stable as I moved from stall to stall, saying good morning to each horse. Mr. Jenkins stuck his head around the door of his ranch office.

"I swear you could tell me what each one of them is thinking," he said with gruff admiration.

"Well," I began, taking on the challenge, "Butterscotch has asked for an extra helping of oats in her feed pail. Pepper would like a thorough mane and tail brushing." I added in a whisper, "He's hoping to impress the new mare." Mr. Jenkins smiled.

"And Caboose, here," I said, stroking the oldest of the bunch on his wrinkled muzzle, "is wishing he still had his handsome teeth."

A rumbling chuckle burst from Mr. Jenkins, and he turned away with a wave. "Ah, go on, Dacey! Soon you'll have me believing it!"

"It's all true!" I called after him as I made my way to Ginger's stall. "Every word! Isn't it, girl?" I nuzzled Ginger's nose with my own, my heart warming. "You know, don't you?"

I swear, she did. I could see the understanding in the pools of her eyes. I breathed in, relishing the sweet scent of hay and warm horse—my favorite smells in the entire world. Then I set to work, brushing Ginger until her russet coat gleamed velvet, and saddling her for our ride, feeling a quiet joy stealing over me. I loved my Saturday mornings at the stables, and Ginger looked forward to our long rides as much as I did.

Right now, she was nuzzling my palm impatiently as I adjusted the length of a stirrup, making me lose my grip on the strap.

"I know, I know." I smiled. "I'm hurrying." She stamped her

right front hoof against the straw-strewn floor, whinnying, and I laughed. "Don't get sore at me. It's Zari who's the late one."

I glanced at my phone as I led Ginger from her stall into the stable yard: 6:32 a.m. Zari should've been here fifteen minutes ago, saddling up the Jenkinses' horse Pepper. We got to the stables before dawn every Saturday to ride. That gave us two hours on the trails before I had to open Pies N' Prattle with Mom at nine o'clock.

I texted Zari a WHERE R U? and seconds later got back a yawning emoji face followed by: SNOOZING IT. C U L8TR.

I rolled my eyes at Ginger. "Zari overslept again." I ruffled her forelock. "Looks like it's just you and me."

I put on my riding helmet and mounted Ginger, smiling as I slid into the saddle with the second nature of having done it a thousand times before. Even without Zari riding Pepper beside me, nothing could dampen my mood. I handled Ginger with a confidence I never felt in the kitchen. It was under the wide expanse of Texas sky, with its whipped-cream clouds, cantering Ginger through the golden prairie, that I felt most myself.

I urged Ginger on faster, nudging her with my heels and feeling her excitement as we broke from a canter into a full gallop, racing past the Jenkinses' longhorns grazing in the fields toward the grove of oaks, walnuts, and elms that marked the edge of the Brazos River.

I slowed Ginger to a walk, steering her toward a serene trail that wound along the water to an old abandoned railroad trestle. We moved under the shade of the live oaks, then started down the embankment toward the water.

Once we were on the flat ground beside the burbling river, I loosened my grip on the reins, lying back in the saddle until I was almost horizontal, taking in the speckling of sky and green branches overhead. Ginger knew this trail as well as I did, and I closed my eyes, knowing she'd lead the way, sure and steady as always.

Suddenly, though, she jerked to a stop, jolting me until I nearly slid sideways out of the saddle. "Easy, girl!" I soothed Ginger, who was tense and wary, as I scrambled to grab the reins and right myself.

There was a horse blocking the trail, snorting and prancing, looking like he might rise up on his hind legs any second. I recognized him as Flash—the Jenkinses' newest gelding, unbroken and feisty enough to throw anybody who showed even the slightest hint of fear. Horses are like that—they know weak riders from strong ones.

This rider, though—a boy about my age, wearing a Stetson hat—wasn't shirking at Flash's tantrum. A laugh broke from him, confident and rascally. I could only make out his silhouette against the morning light.

"Your horse shouldn't sneak up on people like that," came his teasing voice.

"*My* horse!" I stiffened. "*Your* horse spooked mine! You've no business being on this trail with an unbroken horse. It's not safe. He's completely unpredictable."

"Not when I'm riding him," the boy replied. "And there's room for two horses on this trail, if they're going the same direction."

I started to argue, but I knew what he said was true. Zari and I rode this trail together all the time. Only I didn't want to admit it to this stranger. His brashness had me on the defensive.

"I'm not." I prodded Ginger to get her to step around Flash. "I'm going the other way."

"Of course you are." He laughed again. "You always go your own way, Dacey Culpepper Biel."

I froze, staring at him. How did he know my name? I opened my mouth to ask, but then he swept his hat from his head. I caught my breath. Espresso eyes were set in an angular bronze face under thick, jet black brows. His black hair fell to his chin in disheveled waves. He had a rugged cuteness, but something about his face nagged at me. He looked familiar. "Who . . . ?"

"You don't remember?" He grinned. "It's me. Chayton."

My heart plunged to my toes as my memory of the ten-year-old Chayton meshed with the twelve-year-old boy before me. My expression must have revealed my dismay because Chayton gave a wry nod.

"Yup, it's me. The boy you swore you never wanted to set eyes on again as long as you lived."

My fist tightened around Ginger's reins. "I was covered head to toe in purple pie filling at the time."

His eyes glinted maddeningly. "Hey, purple is your color."

I frowned. "And your teasing is just as badly timed as always."

"Aw, come on. You can't still be angry about that, can you? Two years is too long to hold a grudge."

"Not if it's justified," I muttered.

Chayton shook his head. "You never could admit to being wrong, Dace," he said softly.

"What?" I glared at him, every muscle in my body tensing. "You don't even kn—" I swallowed down the rest, knowing it was pointless to argue. But I got even madder when I caught Chayton's amused expression, as if he thought my indignation was great entertainment. I whipped Ginger around in the direction of the stables. "I'm heading back."

"Don't leave on my account." Chayton urged Flash past us, setting his hat back on his head. "I ran Flash hard already. I'll go. You stay." He tipped his hat to me, a gentlemanly gesture I was sure he'd learned from his grandpa. "Good to see you, Dace."

That last part he said quieter, and some of the mischievous glint left his eyes, replaced with—what? Regret? No. It wasn't possible. Not with Chayton. Still, my face flushed, and I was glad he'd spurred Flash into a gallop and wouldn't notice.

Ginger craned her neck to watch Flash and Chayton until they disappeared from view. Then she gave me a pointed look and snorted.

"Don't look at me like that." I avoided her gaze as I walked her farther down the trail. "He started it." I blew out a breath. "I knew this was going to happen. That the second I saw him, he'd do something to annoy me."

I wished that Ginger was capable of nodding in agreement. But then I wasn't sure she *would*, even if she could. Animals—especially horses—were the best listeners, but I had a sneaking suspicion they harbored plenty of opinions of their own. Ginger was my sounding board, but also, sometimes, my conscience. Now, she simply steadied her gaze on the river bend. We rode in silence and, listening to the burbling water and the distant lowing of cattle, I settled into calm again.

I stared out at the river—beautiful to me even in its muddied olive color. Okay, maybe it *was* a lot to hold a two-year grudge. But seeing Chayton again had brought back the embarrassment I'd felt all those years ago, and that wasn't an easy thing to shake.

I knew what Zari would say if she were here. No doubt I'd hear it later when I told her what had happened. "You're not going to be able to avoid him completely," or "Maybe he just wants to be friends."

It was true; I'd have to see Chayton at school. But I didn't need any more friends. I was good, just the way things were. I clicked my tongue and swung Ginger away and up the riverbank and into the flat prairie grass. I was done thinking about it.

"Come on, girl." I nudged Ginger into a gallop. "Let's break it wide open."

Ginger's head dropped, her neck and legs pumping as she gave a great burst of speed. I laughed, exhilarated, as we tore through the field, and the wind whipped away every trace of Chayton Freedell.

When I reached Pies N' Prattle, I saw Dad's bicycle leaning against the shop's porch. I smiled. Most Saturdays, Dad held morning hours at his Paws and Claws veterinary clinic. Because he owned his own business, like Mom, he worked hard, but while Mom always took her work with her—giving advice and/ or pies to clients when she ran into them at the grocery store or the salon—Dad was better about leaving his work at the clinic.

When Dad didn't have any morning clients I'd find him in the pie shop, helping Mom in the back or, if business was slow like it had been recently, doing the Sudoku puzzle in the *Bonnet Times*. I loved having his laid-back presence there, especially if it meant I could challenge him to a game of rummy instead of baking pies.

"Hey, Honeybee." Dad grinned at me over his reading glasses as I entered the shop.

"Hey!" I said.

I stepped toward him—then stopped when a sticky-sweet voice crooned, "Why, Dacey Culpepper Biel. You've shot up two feet since I last set eyes on you! And what luscious hair!"

I turned to see Julip Freedell beaming at me from the couch where she was sitting beside Mom. From her flawlessly matched tunic and capri pants to her sleek chignon, Chayton's mom looked every bit the TV star she was. "Nice to see you, Mrs. Freedell," I offered quickly and politely, hoping that was all that would be needed for me to escape to my dad.

"I was just chatting with your mom about the Bonnet County Fair. It's going to be the best fair yet," Julip gushed. "It'll take work, of course. Some banners and white twinkle lights for Main Street." She tapped a fingernail against her glossy lips and consulted a quilted floral-patterned planner in her lap. "This fairy godmother's going to need a whole lot of mice to make over this pumpkin patch. But we can do it!"

Mom smiled indulgently. "It will be wonderful for Bonnet," she said.

"What would be even more wonderful"—Julip leaned toward Mom—"is if that Heartstring Pie recipe could be found in time for the fair. Folks would come here in droves for a taste of it. And I—I mean, we—could stream the entire experience live. The ratings would be through the roof."

Mom's smile tightened almost imperceptibly. "Now that *would* take magic."

"Magic—bah!" Julip dismissed the idea with a crinkle of her nose. "It takes digging and research is all. I've got people working on it already."

I felt a tug of unease in my gut. "Working on finding the recipe?" I asked.

She smiled. "Of course! The Bonnet library's archives are a rat's nest, but I've got a *Prairie Living* historian combing through them right now. We're bound to find something . . ." She began humming a jaunty tune, then registered Mom's silence and added, "Of course I'll share anything we find with you, Edie. Right away."

"Mmm-hmm," Mom said flatly, her expression troubled.

"But, in all honesty, I've never been completely sure GG Hazel wanted that recipe found."

"Well. I doubt she would've said 'no' to the fortune it could make this shop today, when you need it most." Julip pressed her hand over Mom's. "Savvy businesswomen know when to seize profitable opportunities, don't they?"

I frowned, and Mom caught sight of it and sent me a warning look. Then the shop's front bell dinged and in came Mrs. Gonzalez with the crying Marco.

Mom stood. "Julip, I have to go."

"So do I!" Julip scooped up her planner. "Off to Joe's Hardware for paint samples." She blew a kiss to Mom and breezed out the door before she registered my grimace.

I collapsed into a chair beside Dad. "Seriously?" I grumbled. "Julip Freedell hasn't set foot in this town in two years. She doesn't care about our business. She cares about entertaining her audience!"

Mom glanced at us as she scooped Marco from Mrs. Gonzalez's arms.

"That's not fair, Dace." Mom swayed as she patted Marco's back. "Julip left Bonnet not long after she divorced Chayton's dad. She needed a job to help take care of Chayton. Chayton's grandpa wanted her to move back to the ranch, but he and Julip didn't see eye to eye. They haven't been on speaking terms, but now they're trying to start fresh for Chayton's sake."

"Oh." Some of my annoyance dimmed. "I didn't know that."

Dad leaned toward me, whispering, "Haven't I always told you? Best never to start a debate with your mother. She could argue an owl out of a tree."

"Heard that!" Mom called playfully from the other side of the room.

Dad jerked his thumb in her direction, his eyebrows lifted.

"Saw that, too!" Mom said, although her back was to us.

Dad chuckled. "There's no reckoning with Culpepper women. They're a force."

Mom handed a calmer Marco back to Mrs. Gonzalez, then walked over to Dad and planted a kiss on his cheek. "Wiser words were never spoken, my love."

I couldn't even bring myself to roll my eyes at my parents' mushiness. I'd known my whole life that their love was the real deal, and I admired it too much to poke fun at it. Still, I often wondered how two people so totally different could be so happy together.

"What about what Julip said about the Heartstring Pie recipe?" I asked Mom. "You don't think she'll find anything, do you?"

Mom sighed. "You know how many people have tried and failed to find that recipe. The summer I turned eight, Mr. Lewis dug under his entire bean crop, claiming Hazel told him where the recipe was buried in a dream. Julip won't find anything, and if she does, I trust she'll tell me." She nodded at Hazel's picture on the wall. "GG Hazel always believed in giving people chances. She said second chances were like second helpings of pie . . ."

"Soothing to the soul," Dad and I finished for her.

Mom smiled. "Exactly."

Dad's cell buzzed and he glanced down at the text, then stood. "Gotta go. It's Clover's time and looks like the baby's breech. Poor sweetheart."

Clover was the Johnsons' goat, and Dad's heartfelt concern toward her—and all his patients—made him Bonnet's favorite (and only) veterinarian. And I shared Dad's love of animals. "Can I come help?" I asked eagerly.

Dad nodded at the same time Mom said, "I thought you could help me with some pies . . ."

I was grateful when Dad said, "The animals are calmer when Dacey's with me, Edie. She has a way with them."

I blushed at Dad's compliment. It was funny how, when it came to animals, I'd always known what to do. It wasn't just with Ginger and the Jenkinses' horses. When I spoke to animals and petted them, they responded to my voice and touch, leaning into me, breathing easier, relaxing. It made me think that maybe I could be a vet someday, like Dad. For now, though, I could only think of cuddling with Clover and *not* having to make pies.

"Please, Mom? It's the miracle of life," I offered sweetly.

Mom burst out laughing. "Co-conspirators. The both of you. Out!" She pointed to the door.

"Quick, before she changes her mind," Dad whispered loudly enough for Mom to launch a dish towel at his head.

"You're baking with me tomorrow!" Mom called after me. "We need some new recipes for the fair."

"Tomorrow!" I promised as Dad and I made our break for it. I hopped onto the handlebars of Dad's bike, even though we both knew I was nearly too tall for it, and we headed off.

With the sun in my face and Dad whistling "A Bicycle Built for Two," I could almost forget my encounters with Chayton and his mom. Still, it was hard to forget the CLOSED and FOR SALE signs we passed every few feet.

Maybe Mom was right. Maybe Julip Freedell deserved the chance to breathe life back into Bonnet. As for Chayton? The jury was still out.

Chapter Three

Mom spun me around while I kept my eyes closed. Anyone watching might've thought we looked crazy, but Mom was a sucker for family tradition, so here we were playing pie roulette.

"I still don't believe GG Hazel did this," I said, dizzy, when Mom finally stopped spinning me.

"She most certainly did." Mom walked me toward the shop's refrigerator. "Whenever she wasn't sure what kind of pie to bake, she let serendipity lead the way."

Mom opened the fridge and I swept my hand from side to side. The first thing my fingertips touched was a pile of soft, plump berries.

I peeked with one eye. "Blackberries."

"A perfect first ingredient." Mom grinned as she pulled them from the fridge. "Now for the second." She spun me again, this time pointing me toward the kitchen counter.

My fingers landed on a tin—I opened my eyes—of unsweetened baking cocoa. I raised a skeptical eyebrow, but Mom looked delighted.

"See?" She squeezed my shoulder. "The trick is not to overthink it. Let instinct guide you and don't fight the call of your baking genes."

"Um . . ." I stared at the blackberries and chocolate, waiting for my baking genes to impart wisdom. Nothing came. "Mom?" I turned to her helplessly.

"Don't panic." She hoisted a picnic basket full of apple-cheddar pies onto her hip. "I have to run these pies over to the Sunday Bruncher's Book Club. The shop won't open for another hour. Plenty of time for you to experiment. I'll be back in twenty minutes."

"That's twenty minutes too long." I picked up the tin of

baking cocoa. "Remember the last time you left me alone to mix ingredients? I bet GG Hazel never confused balsamic vinegar with vanilla extract."

"That was my fault," Mom countered. "The bottles weren't labeled—"

"Or set a marshmallow sweet potato pie on fire . . ."

Mom waved her hand dismissively. "You were only ten." She blew me a kiss. "Love you. See you soon!"

"Mom—"

The kitchen door swung shut. I was alone, staring at my two ingredients without an iota of inspiration. I leaned against the counter, torn between not wanting to try (and fail) and not wanting to let Mom down. Finally, I had the flicker of an idea.

I melted a stick of butter in the microwave, then set about crushing up the homemade Mexican hot chocolate cookies Mrs. Gonzalez had given Mom in thanks for her first full night of sleep since Marco's birth. (She credited Mom's lavender honey pie.) After mixing the butter and cookie crumbs together, I pressed them into the bottom of two deep-dish pie pans.

Next, I poured a generous pile of cocoa powder into a pot of water and brought it to a simmer. Once it cooled, I stirred in some cream until I had a silky-smooth ganache. The kitchen filled with the scent of warm chocolate, and I breathed in deep, thinking that, if I did nothing else right today, at least I had made a decent chocolate sauce.

I scooped the blackberries into the pie pans, then poured the ganache sauce over them. *Not too bad*, I thought, my hopes lifting. I'd come this far. Maybe I could do this after all.

I opened the oven door, then carefully lifted the pies, balancing one in each hand, ready to set them in to bake.

That's when it happened. The kitchen door flew open, catching me in the back so that I stumbled forward while the pies tipped, dumping their entire contents all over my front.

I gasped as purple and brown mush ran down my shirt and jeans, soaking through my clothes. "Mom!" I shrieked, thinking that she must've rushed back inside, having forgotten something, and slammed into me with the door in her hurry.

"Not Mom," an all-too-familiar voice said with a chuckle.

No. Way. This could not be happening. I turned slowly to face Chayton Freedell.

"I'm . . . really sorry," he choked out, but there was a merry light in his eyes. He glanced around the kitchen. "Paper towels." He grabbed some from the counter. "*Lots* of paper towels."

He hurried toward me with a wad of them in his hand.

"Wha—how did you even get in here?" I sputtered, snatching the towels from him and making a pathetic attempt to wipe at the goop clinging to every inch of me.

He shrugged. "The shop door was open. I thought—"

"The sign on the door says 'Closed.'" My voice was getting louder.

"My mom sent me over to drop off some stuff for your mom. Some ideas for renovating the shop, I guess."

I gritted my teeth. "We're. Not. Renovating."

"Well." The corner of his lips curled into an impish grin. "I don't know about that. If you went with a purple motif, you wouldn't even have to change much." He motioned to the purple pie splatters on the floor, walls, and counter. His lips twitched in their attempt to hold in his amusement, and my face flamed.

This was too much. Suddenly I was ten years old, covered head to toe in pie at the county fair. Chayton Freedell had done it again, and there was no way this was accidental. It just wasn't possible.

He reached his hand toward my cheek, his eyes glinting. "Um . . . you've got a little something on your face—" He burst out laughing, and I combusted.

"Shut. Up." I hissed. "This. Isn't. Funny."

He held up his hands. "It is kind of funny. Just a little bit—"

"You did this on purpose!" I yelled, unleashing the fury that had been steadily building in me. "Just like in the parade!"

Chayton's eyes widened. "Wait. What? I didn't—"

"I've never done a thing to you! And you!" I jabbed a finger into his chest. "You go out of your way to humiliate me!"

Chayton's smile faded, and for a second he looked as if I'd struck him. A small part of me—a very small part—wondered if I was overreacting. I knew I flashed fire only to regret it later once I'd regained my composure. But I was too far gone now.

"Hang on a sec, Dace," Chayton tried, "I didn't mean any of this. It was an accident, that's all. Honestly—"

I whirled away from him toward the counter, where my hand found a pile of the blackberry pie filling. My fist closed around it, and my arm cocked back.

And I launched the pie filling right at Chayton.

It landed with a satisfying *Squish!* square on his face.

"There!" I cried, triumphant. "How does it feel?"

It was at that moment that Mom swung through the kitchen door. Her eyes flicked from the mess to my face to Chayton's, her expression horrified. "Dacey! What on earth?"

"It's my fault, Miss Edie," Chayton said, wiping pie from his eyes. "We had a small collision and we were just about to start cleaning up."

Mom handed Chayton a paper towel. "Don't you worry about cleaning up, Chayton. I ran into your mom outside. She's looking for you. Something about needing help with loading paints into her car?"

Chayton sighed and a trace of sadness crossed his face. It was gone in a blink, though, instantly replaced by a chipper expression. "I'll get going, then." He used his finger to wipe a dollop of pie filling off his cheek, then popped his finger into his mouth.

He grinned at me. "Didn't even need to be baked to be delicious." I scowled, and he shrugged. "Okay, okay. I got the message." He used the paper towel to wipe the rest of the pie clean from his face, then looked back at me, giving me his easy, maddening smile. "You've always had the temper, Dace. I didn't know you had such great aim."

His laughter lingered in the kitchen after he'd disappeared through the door, making me even madder. "I should've hit him with a whole pie!"

"Dacey!" Mom chided me. "I'm not gone five minutes and you wage a war?"

"He dumped the pie all over me. *Again!* On purpose!" I grabbed paper towels to wipe the counter while Mom filled the mop bucket with water.

She glanced at me skeptically. "Now why would he do something like that?" Her voice, as always, was infuriatingly calm and rational. She gasped then, feigning horror. "Maybe . . . he's a member of the Illuminati, his sole purpose to seek out and destroy the life of one Dacey Culpepper Biel!"

I snorted. "Omigod, Mom. The Illuminati? *Please* stop." I laughed, despite myself. "You sound completely ridiculous!"

"Oh?" She raised an eyebrow in my direction. "I do?"

I groaned but refused to concede her point. "You don't know Chayton like I do. He's, he's—" *Obnoxiously blasé about everything,* I thought, *and he makes me feel ridiculous in my seriousness.* Only, I didn't want to admit any of that.

"He's new to town." Mom handed me the mop. "And he's Julip Freedell's son, and like it or not, Julip wields a lot of influence."

"Or not," I mumbled under my breath.

"It wouldn't be wise to make an enemy of Chayton. It wouldn't be generous of spirit, either." Mom was doing that no-nonsense thing she was so good at.

I dropped my head and focused on swishing the mop back and forth across the floor.

Mom began rolling out some dough. "When you're finished mopping, go on home to clean up. We'll try another pie later, after you've had the chance to simmer down some."

There was a finality in her tone that said that the discussion was over and that, even though she wasn't angry, she'd expected better of me.

Before I left, I scooped up a fingerful of the pie filling from the counter and tried it. Chayton had been right about that, at least. The filling tasted delicious. Only I'd managed to screw it up anyway. Typical.

When I got home, I tried to sneak past Dad's office, but since the window of his examination room faced Main Street, and I resembled a mutant blueberry, it didn't work.

He stuck his head out his open window, trying but failing to hide his smile. "Need an appointment?" he asked. "I have an opening in fifteen minutes."

Whenever I needed to talk to Dad when he was at work, he

booked me in for an appointment. When I was smaller, I used to invent ailments for myself and pretend to be a horse, or a cat, or dog. Then Dad would set me up on the exam table and listen to my complaints about a squabble with Zari or an awful homework assignment, and then offer a diagnosis and cure.

"You're suffering from acute argumentitis," he said when Zari and I fought over sharing a toy. "I prescribe ice cream sundaes from The Creamery, pronto."

I'd outgrown pretending to be an animal, but hadn't outgrown our office consults, so I nodded, saying, "Book me for the appointment. I'll be back when I'm de-blackberried."

A minute later, I caught sight of myself in the bathroom mirror. I might've easily passed for Violet Beauregarde after she eats the three-course chewing gum in *Charlie and the Chocolate Factory.*

It took a serious scrubbing to rid myself of the sticky purple sludge, and the hot shower soaked up some of my anger, too. By the time I'd dried off and dressed in fresh clothes, I was replaying the events of the morning and second-guessing everything

I'd said and done to Chayton. It didn't help that my phone was chiming every few seconds with texts from Zari.

JUST SAW CHAYTON, the first one read. U DID *NOT* HIT HIM WITH A PIE?!?

This was followed by half a dozen more texts demanding details and/or pics, but when I didn't respond, my phone went eerily silent. This could only mean one thing: Zari had gotten the entire story from Chayton himself. This was not comforting, especially given Zari's penchant for sensationalism, but I wasn't ready to talk to her yet. Even though she was my best friend, her mind worked like a reporter's, and I wasn't in the mood to give the in-depth play-by-play that would satisfy her need for detail.

Sometimes, I just needed an impartial ear, and the best one I knew of was Dad's. I used the private door that led from our kitchen into the clinic's recovery room. This was where Dad kept his inpatients. Today, there were two: Calico, one of Ms. Aberdine's many cats, diagnosed with a broken toe, and Atlas, Mr. Walker's chocolate lab, recovering from back surgery. I stopped in front of Calico's and Atlas's kennels, whispering "hello"s to them and stroking their noses. I realized, then, that in comparison to the days the two of them had had, mine might not have been so terrible.

Soon, Dad waved me into his examination room. "Want a ride?" he asked with a chuckle, nodding toward the exam table. It was equipped with a hydraulic lift that could raise and lower it like an elevator; I'd loved it as a little kid.

"Not today." I sank into the chair across from his desk.

Dad gave a low whistle. "Must be serious."

His voice was quiet and inviting, and within seconds, I was recounting everything that had happened at Pies N' Prattle with Chayton.

"He really gets under your skin, doesn't he?" Dad remarked.

"Only since forever." I plucked at the small fibers on the fabric of the chair.

"Your mom had a similar experience with a schoolmate once," Dad said. "He drove her crazy. Was always slipping frogs into her backpack and copycatting her ideas for book reports and school projects."

"I didn't know that. How annoying. She must've been dying to get him to quit."

"Oh, she was, and she finally came up with a solution."

I leaned forward. "What did she do?" I asked, envisioning some great comeuppance.

Dad grinned. "She married him."

"Dad! *So* not helpful!" I rolled my eyes, but couldn't help laughing at the same time.

He shrugged innocently. "You're right. Sorry. *But* you're never marrying anyone anyway, because no one will ever be worthy enough of my approval."

"Um, hello? Twenty-first century? I don't need parental approval." I laughed at Dad's faux-hurt expression. "But . . . can we be serious for a sec?"

"You got it." Dad saluted me, then steadied his gaze. "Seriously, your mom's been downplaying the situation, but the truth is, Bonnet's depressed. You know other businesses are closing, but Pies N' Prattle is struggling, too."

My stomach clenched. "We have our regulars."

"Most of whom eat for free. Your mother probably gives away four times more pies than she sells. And she won't hear a word about it. She says GG Hazel never charged a cent for her Heartstring Pie, and as far as she's concerned, pies that are for mending shouldn't come with price tags."

"I didn't know that," I said, though I wondered if I knew more than I'd admitted to myself. There'd been plenty of occasions when I'd heard Mom whisper, "On the house" to customers, as she'd done with Mr. Jenkins the other day. I guess I'd assumed that for every customer who hadn't paid for pie, there'd been others who had. "But Dad, would it be such a horrible thing if the shop closed eventually? It can't stay open forever. I mean, it's been open for decades and Mom runs it now, but what about later on?"

Dad stared at me, eyes wide, as if I'd just informed him that the universe was coming to an end. He cleared his throat awkwardly, and I realized with a shock that what I'd just said had made him uncomfortable. "Dacey, have you ever watched your mom when she closes shop at night? *Really* watched?" I shook my head. "Just before she leaves, she puts her palm against the picture of GG Hazel in the dining room, and she says, 'More hearts tomorrow. I promise, GG.'"

"But GG Hazel would understand if something happened with the shop that was beyond Mom's control—"

"It's not GG Hazel. It's your mom." Dad leaned toward me, more serious than I'd ever seen him. "Your mom's heart is in that shop. Oh, she shares her heart with us, sure. But it really beats to the rhythm of Pies N' Prattle. Just like GG's heart did. If the shop closed, your mom would feel like she was letting her grand-mother down."

I swallowed thickly. There was something else Dad wasn't saying, something that made my own heart quicken with dread. I knew why he didn't want to say it aloud, because it would be too much pressure and too early in my life for it. But I saw the truth clearly, filling the spaces between his words. Mom was hoping that, someday, Pies N' Prattle would belong to me. The thought terrified me. How could Mom expect me to run an entire pie shop when I couldn't even manage to bake a single decent pie?

"Dad, Mom helps people. Fixes their problems sometimes. But she can't fix an entire town."

Dad laughed. "After sixteen years of marriage, I've learned not to put anything past your mom. And now that Julip Freedell's here, who knows what the two of them will accomplish?"

He checked his watch and grabbed his stethoscope from the counter. "I hate to leave you in the doldrums, but duty calls." He paused with one hand on the door. "Diagnosis: Chronic Chaytonconfusis." He scribbled something on his prescription pad, tore it off, and handed it to me. Then he kissed my forehead. "See you at dinner, Honeybee."

The door clicked closed. Dad hadn't given me any real solutions, but I felt better after having talked to him. I glanced down at the prescription in my hand and laughed.

It read: *Avoid all boys until you're thirty (except your father, of course).*

Chapter Four

Dad's advice was meant as a joke, but within ten minutes of walking into Bonnet Middle School on Monday morning, I was seriously considering following it. For the rest of my life. The first two boys I saw in the front hallway were JC and Tad, who ducked and held up their hands.

"Don't throw anything at us, Dacey!" Tad cried mockingly. "Have mercy!"

By the time I reached the lockers, Nick and Dante had commented on my "fastball," and Greg had joked about me pitching for the baseball team. When my friends Bree and Maria fell into step beside me, the two of them were grinning like cats at an all-you-can-eat canary buffet.

"You sure know how to make a reunion memorable, Dace!" Maria laughed, tossing her long brown braid over one shoulder. Then her cell phone rang, and she answered, shifting into a string of rapid Spanish. When she hung up, she groaned. "That was Juliana wanting pics." Maria was always getting annoyed at her gossipy older sister. "I told her not a chance." Then she added, her eyes gleaming with curiosity and amusement, "You don't have any pics, do you?"

"Maria!" I stopped in front of my locker. "So . . . who else knows besides Juliana?" When my question was met with a long silence, the truth settled in. "Everyone knows, don't they?" It wasn't that surprising, considering the wildfire speed with which news spread in Bonnet, but I hadn't been prepared for Chayton and me to be the talk of the student body.

"Maybe not everyone," Bree said optimistically, her blue eyes bright beneath her blond bangs. "Some kids don't read the Bonnet Buzz. One or two kids . . . probably."

My hand froze on my combination lock. If the story of my pie assault was in the Bonnet Buzz, that could only mean one thing. I pulled up this morning's edition of the school paper on my phone and scrolled through the articles, muttering, "Tell me she didn't . . ."

But there it was, Zari's Bonnet Buzz column with the headline: PIE IN THE EYE.

> The rivalry between Dacey Culpepper Biel and Chayton Freedell is alive and well after a two-year hiatus. Who will win this time? Only pie will tell . . .

I grimaced, and Maria and Bree exchanged doleful glances. Before they could say a word, Zari rounded the corner and greeted us with an über-cheery, "Morning, y'all!"

"Zari!" I held my screen up to her face. "The entire column? Really?"

"Oh, you know it was too good to pass up." Zari grinned, completely unflustered. "Isn't it funny? One of my better pieces, I think."

"It was." Bree nodded appreciatively. She was the most obliging of our group—slow to criticize and quick to compliment. "I especially like the 'Whatever happens with these two promises to be *berry* entertaining' line."

Zari beamed proudly. "Thanks."

Then Bree turned to me, adding, "And Chayton *did* say you were a commendable adversary."

"Huh. I missed that quote." A second later, I had a sinking realization. "Wait . . . You quoted him directly?"

Zari nodded. "He gave me a full interview. It was great!" When I frowned, she threw her arms around me. "Come on, Dace, the whole thing *was* funny, and I was desperate for material. It was between you and Mrs. Lacey's gallbladder surgery. Did you want the entire student body to die of boredom, or to start their Mondays with a smile?"

I paused, weighing my affection for Zari against my annoyance with the story. In the end, Zari won out, like she always did. Even though she sometimes took her nose for news too far, she never did it with the intention of harming anyone. As I reread the article, I remembered the stunned look on Chayton's berry-splattered face. I'd probably looked just as ridiculous. It *was* funny in retrospect. "I do wish I'd taken a pic." I giggled, and Zari's expression broke into one of relief.

"That would've been priceless," Zari said as the bell rang.

My friends and I headed in different directions for our first-period classes. As I stepped into Spanish, I was surprised to see Chayton walking into the classroom two doors down. Of course I'd known he'd be at school, only I hadn't mentally prepared myself yet for the fact that I'd be seeing him every day.

My eyes lingered a millisecond too long, and he looked up to catch my gaze. He grinned and waved. "Been practicing your windup for lunchtime? I heard chicken pot pie's on the menu."

I dropped my eyes and hurried into class, my cheeks burning. As I sat down at my desk, Caroleen, one of the most popular girls in school, leaned toward me.

"There are plenty of boys I'd love to throw pies at, too," she said. "But I can't believe you'd mess with a face as adorable as

Chayton's." Several of the girls seated around us laughed in agreement.

I hoped that would be the last I'd hear about Chayton for a while, but then Principal Carter began the morning announcements over the loudspeaker. After welcoming Chayton back to Bonnet and into our school, Mr. Carter continued, "I also have Chayton's mother, our very own celebrity Julip Freedell, here in the office for a special announcement."

My stomach sank. Everyone else around me sat up straighter in their seats, keen to hear what came next.

"Good morning, y'all!" Julip's voice crooned over the speaker. "The Bonnet County Fair is less than two weeks away, and I'm looking for hardworking volunteers to help me make over our beloved Main Street for the special day. The makeover will be filmed live, and anyone who volunteers will have a chance to appear on my special episode of *Prairie Living*. Sign-up sheets will be posted in the cafeteria. Please sign up and help us bring back Bonnet's beauty!"

Applause and excited chatter erupted in the room. Everyone was talking over one another, saying they were going to be the first to volunteer and asking what colors filmed the best. It was reality TV pandemonium.

I sank deeper into my seat as Señora Gomez called our class to order. Chayton and Julip Freedell were the talk of the town, and it was becoming clearer by the second that there was no place I could go to escape them.

After school, I called Mom and asked her if I could skip my afternoon shift at Pies N' Prattle so I could ride Ginger. Mom wasn't thrilled, but finally she relented.

"Ride whatever it is out of your system today and you'll come to the shop fresh tomorrow," she said.

I hurried down Main Street, my mood darkening when I caught sight of Julip Freedell. She was walking out of the Bonnet library alongside an unfamiliar man. Their heads were bent over a piece of paper, and they were whispering excitedly. I remembered what she'd said about digging through the library's archives for clues about the Heartstring Pie recipe, and curiosity made me pause to listen to their conversation.

"I'll get this back to the ranch right away," Julip was saying. "No need to share this with anyone else just yet."

A protective anger burbled under my skin. *What if she actually found something about GG Hazel?* Now she was planning to keep it to herself? No way was I letting that happen.

"My father has some old maps of Bonnet," Julip continued, "and I remember an old oak tree that—"

"Hi, Ms. Freedell!" I blurted, making her jump as I walked right up to her. My eyes zeroed in on the piece of paper she was holding. "Do you have some news about my great-grandmother?" I added a little emphasis on *my* just to make a point.

"Uh . . ." A faint blush crept over her cheeks, and she glanced down at the paper. "Why, yes! Yes I do! I was just going to run it over to your mother."

Yeah, right, I thought, but what I said was, "She'll be thrilled. Can I see?"

"Of course!"

Julip handed me the paper. It was a Xerox of an old newspaper clipping, an article in the *Bonnet Times* announcing Hazel Culpepper's passing at the age of fifty-nine. The article had quotes from Bonneters recounting all the ways Hazel had helped them through the years and how they'd miss her. Three sentences toward the end of the article made my pulse thrum:

> According to Mabel Culpepper, Hazel's bereaved daughter, Hazel hid her famous Heartstring Pie recipe just days before her passing. Hazel's last words were, "The secret to the sweetest of pies is hidden in the heart of Bonnet." One has to wonder, was this a clue to the recipe's whereabouts?

My brow furrowed. What did Hazel mean by "the heart of Bonnet"? Did she mean a symbolic heart or a literal one? And *was* she talking about Heartstring Pie?

"Has your mother ever mentioned this to you before, Dacey?" Julip asked, an urgency in her voice. "Anything about a Bonnet heart?" She stared so intently at the paper, I was surprised her eyes didn't burn holes in it.

"No," I said honestly. Then, for a little bit of fun, I added, "But there *is* that heart painted on the barn by Tootsie's pigsty." Even if GG Hazel had meant a real heart, there was *no* way she'd hide her pie recipe in a pigsty. *No. Way.*

"At Mr. Victor's?" Julip practically bounced with excitement. "Yes, I *do* remember that." She nodded to the man beside her, and together they hurried to Julip's truck. Julip called to me over her shoulder, "Be sure to give your mother that article. Have her call me if anything—*anything*—comes to her mind."

I watched Julip's truck speed off in the direction of Mr. Victor's, and I giggled, imagining her digging through the muck in her high heels. As I resumed my walk to the Jenkins ranch, I couldn't stop thinking about the article. What if Hazel's words really *were* a clue? And hadn't Julip mentioned something about an old oak tree? What did that mean? By the time I turned down the Jenkinses' lane, I had an itching to go search for hearts around Bonnet myself.

I looked up and saw Chayton riding Flash out of the stables. For a moment I felt a tug of empathy for him. His mom always seemed to be chasing after her next big break, a more perfect version of life. But where did that leave Chayton?

Then I shook the thought away, reminding myself that I wasn't friends with Chayton, and I didn't want to be friends with him, so there was no point in thinking about him at all.

At least I'd seen him head out on Flash. I'd make sure I took Ginger in a different direction, so Chayton and I didn't run into each other like we had last time.

When I reached Ginger's stall and peeked inside, my heart froze in my chest.

"Ginger?" I whispered. My blood ran icy cold.

She was rolling on her back, whinnying shrilly as if she were in pain. I opened the stall door and tried to urge her to her feet, but she refused to stand, and her coat was slick with sweat.

I'd seen these symptoms before in some of my dad's horse patients. It was colic. I was sure of it.

With trembling fingers, I called Dad's emergency cell number, the one he only used for work.

"Dacey?" He picked up on the first ring. "What's wrong?"

"It's Ginger." My voice quivered as I described her symptoms, and I hadn't even gotten through all of them when Dad told me he'd be at the stables in ten minutes. Those ten minutes felt like the longest of my life as I tried in vain to get Ginger to her feet.

Dad drove up just as Mr. Jenkins walked into the stables leading Alamo, his Palomino horse, behind him. I guessed he'd been out checking on his herds, which was what he usually did this time of day.

He tipped his hat at me, but the smile fell from his face when he saw my stricken expression and Dad making a beeline for Ginger's stall. "Trouble brewing?" Mr. Jenkins asked.

"Colic," Dad said. I held my breath watching Dad examine Ginger. He took her pulse and listened to her breathing, and then pressed his stethoscope against her belly. He straightened. "It's spasmodic, so that's good news. I'll give her some Banamine for the pain. And we need to get her out of her stall because I don't want her to hurt herself thrashing."

"You can take her to the corral," Mr. Jenkins said as he and Dad urged Ginger to her feet. "She'll have room to move there."

It took a few minutes of encouragement to get Ginger to the corral, and I knew she was still uncomfortable because of the way she kept swinging her head around to reach her flanks.

"Walking her for ten or fifteen minutes every hour will help move the air in her belly," Dad said.

Mr. Jenkins told us he had to take some calls in his office and to let him know if we needed anything. Dad watched me lead Ginger around the corral once, then twice. Dad nodded his approval. "Keep her moving as long as she's comfortable."

"Okay." My voice wavered, and I must've looked exactly the way I felt, terrified, because Dad wrapped me in his arms.

"I can stay." Even as he said it, his cell phone buzzed, and I knew it was one of his clients, probably needing his help and advice just as badly as I had.

I shook my head. "It's all right, Dad. I can do this."

"I'll come back later to check in on her. Call me ASAP if she seems any worse." He squeezed my hand and left.

I sucked in a breath, then looked deep into Ginger's velvety brown eyes. "Come on, girl," I whispered, urging her forward.

"Let's do this." She was the best nonhuman friend I'd ever had, and I wasn't about to let anything happen to her.

I fell into a rhythm with Ginger, walking around the corral, whispering encouragement and then, when I needed a distraction from my own aching feet, singing whatever random songs popped into my head. Dad and Mom came by two times before sunset—the first time to bring me some dinner and a slice of my favorite pie (Black Forest, still warm from the oven), and the second time to offer to take my place.

"I can't go home," I told them as they exchanged worried glances. "Ginger needs me. I can't leave her."

A warm gust of wind blew up, bringing with it the smell of distant rain.

"There's a front coming through," Dad said. "Rain'll be here soon. Dace—"

"Still staying," I said firmly.

Because they knew me, and because all three of us were

stubborn when it came to these sorts of situations, my parents accepted my answer, gave me one more reassuring group hug, and left, calling over their shoulders that they'd be back later.

The gray wall of slanting rain barreled over the Jenkins ranch an hour later, pelting Ginger and me with stinging drops the size of pennies. Mr. Jenkins had given me one of the ranch's spare slickers when he'd seen the clouds lining up along the horizon, and I pulled it tighter around me now to help shield against the downpour. Soon, though, the rain was falling so torrentially that my boots were filling, too. That was right about the time that Ginger decided to quit, lying down in the middle of the biggest mud puddle in the corral.

"Can't let you do this, girl," I said through the roar of the rain. "Get on up."

She wouldn't budge. Darkness had fallen, and suddenly, I felt utterly alone and exhausted. The pressure behind my eyes warned me that the tears were about to fall. I sank into the mud beside Ginger, not caring about the sludge that soaked through my pants, chilling me to the bone.

"Please," I whispered, "please get up."

I nearly screamed when someone touched my shoulder, and I scrambled backward.

"Dacey, it's me!" A voice came through the shadows, and then a flashlight switched on, illuminating Chayton's face.

"Oh. Hi." Surprised, I struggled to my feet, but I was so tired I couldn't get my balance. Before I could protest, Chayton was helping me, his arms around my waist, steady and firm. His touch felt strangely welcome in the storm before I had time to remember all the reasons it wasn't supposed to be. I felt myself blushing, glad the darkness could cover it.

"Wha—what are you doing here?" I demanded.

"I live here. Remember?" His smile shone in the flashlight's yellow beam, but then his expression turned sober. "Granddad told me about Ginger. How's she doing?"

I wiped at a strand of my drenched, scraggly hair. "The same, I think."

"You've been out here with her for hours."

I nodded, realizing that I didn't even remember seeing

71

Chayton return to the stables with Flash, or anything else that might have been happening while I'd been at Ginger's side. The afternoon and evening hours had blurred together into one unending, weary walk.

Chayton took in my mud-soaked clothes, and I shivered involuntarily. "You're freezing."

"I-I'm fine." My teeth chattered, giving me away.

Chayton shook his head. "I should've come out earlier, only . . ." He smiled again. "I figured you'd be liable to hit me with a mud pie this time."

"I might've," I said, hoping to sound resolute, but the words came out weaker than a kitten's mewl.

Chayton laughed. "Well, I'm here now, so I guess I'll have to take my chances." Together, we got Ginger to her feet again. Chayton reached for Ginger's lead line, but I gripped it tighter. His eyes locked on mine. "Dacey, look. You don't like me. Or, maybe you even hate me, though I'm still trying to puzzle out why . . ." I opened my mouth, but he added, "Point is that I'd like to help. You're worn out, and I'm here. And I'm offering." He paused, letting this sink in. "So?"

I stared at the ground, thinking of the irony of this moment, and how the last person I wanted to help me was the one person offering. I could resume my vow to steer clear of him tomorrow. For tonight, I was too tired to argue, even with Chayton.

So when he slid his hand over the fist I clutched the lead in, I slowly, slowly, let go.

"I can see how much you love her," he said quietly. "I promise to take good care of her."

"I'm not going home," I said firmly.

"I didn't figure you would." He began walking away from me with Ginger, calling over his shoulder, "Granddad put some blankets in Ginger's stall for you and Granny fixed you some hot chocolate. Just go inside and warm up for a little while. That's all."

I hesitated, feeling a pull to stay where I was. But my numb toes and fingers finally won out over my stubbornness, and I slogged my way to Ginger's stall, hoping that Chayton would keep his promise.

Chapter Five

I opened my eyes to sunlight warming my face. I blinked, taking in the straw and dark planked wood surrounding me, then I sat bolt upright, adrenaline jolting me into alertness. I'd been in Ginger's stall all night long!

I scrambled to my feet and rushed outside to find Ginger prancing happily around the corral, all signs of the colic gone.

"Thank goodness you're up." Chayton grinned at me from the Jenkinses' porch, where he sat on the swing, sipping from a steaming cocoa mug. "I couldn't sleep with all your snoring."

"I don't snore," I retorted as I climbed the porch steps. Chayton held a second steaming mug toward me, and I took it gratefully.

The mug was printed with the words, THIS IS WHAT AN AWESOME COWBOY LOOKS LIKE. I raised an eyebrow at Chayton. "Is this yours?"

He shrugged. "Caroleen gave it to me as a welcome back present."

"Caroleen?" Giving little gifts to boys was Caroleen's way of staking her claim to their hearts. My friends and I had watched her do it all through school. Chayton's expression, though, gave no hint as to whether her attempt at charming him had worked. If anything, he seemed as blasé about it as he did everything else.

"After your tough night," he said to me now, "the mug suits you better than me."

He said it teasingly but also with an air of appreciation that made me blush. He scooted over on the swing, and I sat down beside him. "Ginger looks—"

"Better." He nodded. "Your dad came by about an hour ago to check on her. He came by a bunch of times overnight, too, but he wanted to let you sleep." He smiled. "Ginger's on the mend. She'll be fine."

I sighed with relief. "I think that might be the best news I ever heard."

He cocked his head at me. "It was you who made her better, you know."

I scoffed. "Nah. Dad's gotten dozens of horses over colic. He knew what he was doing."

"So did you." His tone was surprisingly sincere. "I watched you with her last night, the way you talked to her. I don't know if it was the sound of your voice or what, but she *got* what you were saying. And you were so relaxed around her, not like—"

He stopped short, but I knew where he'd been going. "Not like I usually am?" I finished the thought. "What, you think I'm mad all the time?" When he didn't answer, I stiffened. "I'm not! But . . . animals are just easier than people sometimes."

"Because they do what you want?" he challenged.

"No!" I laughed, in spite of myself. "Are you kidding? They have minds of their own. You've never seen Ginger misbehaving."

He held up his hands. "Hey, I don't want to pick a fight. I was only saying you're different around her is all."

I swallowed my stubbornness and admitted, "Maybe it *does* calm me down, because it's something I'm good at. My mom's so great at taking care of other people . . . But Ginger's mine to take care of."

"And she trusts you to do it. That's a lot of responsibility, to have someone put their trust in you like that."

"No kidding." I blew out a breath. "Exactly why I'd rather it be a horse than a human." I laughed, but Chayton didn't. I felt his eyes studying me, and suddenly I felt exposed, as if he had a window into all my secret fears. I squirmed, hoping he wouldn't call out what he'd seen. He didn't. Instead, he sat quietly, shifting his eyes to the pasture, as if he wanted to give me a little time.

I took a sip of cocoa. I heard the snuffle of the horses in the stables and the lowing of mourning doves. Beside me, Chayton stifled a hefty yawn. I looked over at him properly for the first time since I'd woken up. There were dark circles under his eyes, and beneath the quilt draped across his shoulders he wore the same clothes he'd had on last night, only now they were as mud-stained as my own.

A surprising thought struck me. "Did you stay up all night?"

He shrugged. "No biggie. I wanted to help. And now Granny's making me biscuits and gravy for breakfast, so it was totally worth it." He turned toward me. "Besides, I was trying to convince you that I'm not the enemy you seem to think I am."

A queasy guilt unsettled my stomach. "Thank you." It came out in a whisper. "I'm grateful for your help."

His eyes widened in feigned shock. "A 'thank you' from Dacey Culpepper Biel? History in the making!"

"Hey!" I elbowed him. "You have no idea how hard that was for me to say."

He held my gaze. "Probably as hard as it is for me to keep my cool when I'm being misjudged." I ducked my head, suddenly self-conscious. "I wonder when you're going to get around to telling me exactly what it is you have against me? It can't be what happened back when we were ten?" My silence answered for me, and he busted out with a laugh. "Dace, that was ages ago!"

I bristled. "Yeah, well. *You* weren't the one who crashed into a table full of pies in front of a hundred people all because of some stupid prank."

"Wait." Realization dawned on his face. "You think I made Ginger throw you on purpose?"

"You did," I blurted, then faltered when I saw his surprise. "Didn't you?"

He gave a small laugh. "I was goofing off during the parade that day, for sure, and I should've quit. But that wasn't what spooked Ginger. I didn't even know what had until after it was all over and Granddad told me. There was a diamondback rattler curled up in the grass near the pie stand. Nobody noticed it until Ginger spooked, and then Granddad caught sight of it. He got rid of it while everybody else was busy helping you out of your pie fix."

I sat in stunned silence. How had I never known about that? All this time, I'd been blaming Chayton for what had happened. "B-but why didn't you tell me? I was so mad and you just let me think it was all your doing."

He shrugged. "I tried to tell you then, but you were so busy yelling at me that I couldn't get a word in edgewise. Then your parents took you home to get you cleaned up, and Mom and I left town a few days later. So I never got the chance to explain."

"Oh." The resentment I'd been harboring toward Chayton slowly crumbled and rearranged itself as regret. I reluctantly pushed the next words from my throat. "My temper . . . It's not one of my best qualities. I shouldn't have jumped to conclusions . . ."

"Even if I *was* a royal pest," he interjected with his impish grin. "I admit it."

I sucked in a breath. "Then I admit that I was wrong and . . . I'm sorry."

He whistled. "I can't believe you actually just said that." His eyes were merry, but there wasn't any sign of gloating in them. "How did it feel?"

"Not too bad," I admitted with a smile. "As far as humble pie goes. But don't push it."

"Not another word." He laughed. "I'm not a fan of holding grudges, so I'm glad we're done with it."

Just then, angry voices, loud though muffled, rose from inside the house.

Chayton shook his head, his cheeks flushing with embarrassment. "Wish my family could do the same," he said quietly. It was the first time I'd ever heard him sound so serious.

"Is that your mom and granddad?" I asked, recognizing the voices.

Chayton nodded. "They argue all the time. The latest is Mom wants Granddad to cut down his favorite oak tree. I'm surprised they didn't wake you."

My ears perked up at his words. "Oak tree?" The one Julip had mentioned yesterday when she hadn't realized I was there?

"Yeah," Chayton said. "It's an ancient oak down by the abandoned railroad trestle. Its trunk divides into two curves, touching again at the top, like the shape of a—"

"Heart?" My pulse pounded.

He nodded. "I figured you probably knew it, since you ride Ginger down there."

I could picture the tree so clearly, now that he'd described it. It was a gnarled old oak that I passed on nearly every ride I took with Ginger. Sometimes I sat in the cradle of its trunk for a break. There was a knothole at the base of the trunk . . . a knothole with a slip of an opening, just big enough to tuck something small, like a piece of paper, inside. My pulse tripled its pace. It wasn't possible, was it?

"I don't even know what bee got in Mom's bonnet about that tree," Chayton continued while my mind whirred, "why she'd want to cut it down. But Granddad said, 'No way.'"

"Why? Is that tree his favorite?"

"Actually it's not," Chayton said. "It was your GG Hazel's favorite. That's what he told Mom earlier when they were *really* yelling. Before you woke up. I guess Hazel liked to picnic there in summertime. She'd have soldiers come with their families, too, to share slices of her Heartstring Pie."

"Then he can't cut it down." Suddenly, I *needed* to see that tree again, and to keep Julip away from it until I did. Only, I couldn't tell Chayton that I suspected the tree might be the hiding place for GG Hazel's pie recipe. Not when I couldn't be sure what he'd do with that information. "It would be bad luck to kill that tree."

"Ha." Chayton smiled in surprise. "I thought that pie curse only applied to baking, and that you didn't buy into it."

"I . . . don't." But I'd hesitated too long, giving away my uncertainty. "Only *I* wouldn't want to end up on the receiving end of that kind of bad luck. That's all. But if that tree was important to GG Hazel the way her pie was, your mom should leave it alone."

Chayton thought about that, then grinned. "Then again, maybe GG Hazel could freeze my mom's tongue or something, just temporarily. Just to get her to quit fighting with Granddad."

I laughed, then sobered. "Is it that bad?"

He shrugged nonchalantly, but his serious face told a different story. "It's always been this way, the two of them going at it. It's why Mom moved us to San Antonio. She loves the spotlight, and Granddad says she felt like Bonnet was too small for her. Too commonplace."

"But Bonnet's smallness is what makes it so great," I said. "People here can really make a difference in each other's lives. Not like in big cities."

Chayton tucked a dark lock behind his ear, looking thoughtful. "Mom thinks the bigger the city, the bigger recognition she'll get. It's why she's so obsessed with this whole Bonnet makeover idea. She's convinced it'll be great for her show."

"Oh." A small part of me felt satisfied knowing that I'd been right not to trust Julip Freedell's motives. But that part was quashed when I saw how unhappy Chayton looked about it.

"Granddad says she's got her priorities mixed up," he continued. "He doesn't think it's healthy for me to travel so much, or that Mom focuses so much on her show's success."

"What do you think?" I asked.

He was quiet for a long moment. "I think . . ." He set down his cocoa cup and threw off his quilt. He grinned, and I got the distinct impression that he wanted to change the subject and was about to use humor—his go-to—as a diversion. "That because you sorely misjudged me for so long, and because I rescued your horse from certain death last night, that maybe you owe me a favor."

I snorted. "Ha. *I* think you exaggerate. But . . . try me."

He cleared his throat with an official air. "Since we've agreed to start our friendship with a clean slate—"

"We have?" I teased.

He fake-glared at me and continued, "And since you've professed your deep and abiding love for Bonnet, I propose you join me in helping with its makeover this Saturday."

I groaned. "Does it have to be that?"

He nudged me. "Almost everybody from school's helping out, and Mom's organizing a big picnic here at the ranch afterward. And when I say picnic, I mean a crawfish-boil-full-band-celeb-appearances type of picnic."

I laughed. "Your mom doesn't do small potatoes, does she?"

"Why do small potatoes when you can have Grammy winners at your beck and call?" He dug the toe of his boot into a groove in the porch boards, looking uncharacteristically sheepish. "Anyway, it would be more fun if you were there."

"Me? Fun?" I cocked my head. "Are you sure you're thinking of the right Dacey? The one that yelled at you and threw pie filling in your face?"

"Definitely that one. Any other Dacey would be way too boring."

My heart gave a flutter. After the way I'd behaved toward him, there were so many other things he might've said about my temper. He was cutting me slack, which I appreciated. "All right. You convinced me. I'm in." I stood up and stepped off the porch. "I better get going. We're already late for school."

"For a worthy cause, though."

Everything he'd done for Ginger came back to me full force, and a wave of gratitude hit me. "Thanks for last night," I said. "I mean it." Then, before he could see me blush, I turned to go.

After stopping at the corral to plant a quick kiss on Ginger's muzzle, I ran for home. My mind was full of clues and oak trees and secrets. *The secret to the sweetest of pies is hidden in the heart of Bonnet.* The words were a steady stream running through my head. I needed to talk to Mom, to give her the article, still in my muddied pocket from yesterday. I needed a plan.

I showered and dressed, then headed for Pies N' Prattle so Mom could write me a note for school explaining my tardiness.

I found Mom on her knees in the shop's kitchen, surrounded by pie pans and bowls. Every cabinet had been emptied onto the floor and countertops.

"Whoa." I surveyed the chaos. "Um . . . spring cleaning?"

Mom glanced up. "Not exactly." She laughed self-consciously. "It's silly, really. I don't know what possessed me to do this. It was something Julip said the other day, and now I can't seem to shake the idea . . ."

"Mom," I said, suddenly intrigued. "What are you talking about?"

She waved her hands. "Oh . . . Julip said that if GG Hazel's Heartstring Pie recipe could be found in time for the fair, that it would draw a huge crowd. At the time, I didn't think much of it. But I couldn't sleep last night, worrying over Ginger and you. So I finally gave up and did some paperwork for the shop." She sighed. "Turns out, our sales figures have gone down seventy-five percent since the Longhorn Loop closed."

My heart fell. *"What?"* That figure was abysmal. "But, our regulars—"

"Only make up twenty percent of our sales. Everything else came from tourists passing through." Mom undid and redid her topknot. "So I started thinking that Julip's notion wasn't such a bad one. I never really looked for the Heartstring Pie recipe before, because I suppose I never really needed it. But this morning I figured, *What the heck? It won't hurt to do some digging.*" She gave another embarrassed laugh. "I had this crazy idea that GG hid the recipe in a compartment in one of the cabinets, but—"

"No luck?"

She shook her head. "No luck."

The sadness in her voice took me by surprise, and I noticed a strain on Mom's face. I remembered what Dad had said about Mom's heart being a part of the shop, and the responsibility she felt for it. How had I not seen—*really* seen—how much the shop meant to her until now? Maybe it was because of how disconnected I felt from the Culpepper talent, or because I'd always thought of the shop as hers and not mine. Seeing her disappointment made my own heart ache and fill with a new determination.

"Mom, you're not being silly." I reached into my pocket and took out the article. "I was actually coming to talk to you about the recipe. Julip found this in the library's archives."

First confusion, and then excitement, crossed Mom's face as she read. When she looked up, her eyes were bright. "What GG Hazel said—"

"I know! It sounds like it means something."

"The heart of Bonnet," Mom murmured. She stood, the energy I was used to seeing on her face returning. "I'm going home. I just had an idea. The wedding chest in my bedroom—"

"The one that belonged to your mom?"

"And GG Hazel before her." Mom clasped my hand. "I haven't opened it in years. Since my wedding. But there's a heart quilted into the inside of the lid—"

I grabbed my backpack. "I'm coming, too."

"Dace, you have school . . ." Mom started, then looked into my eyes. "This is such a crazy idea, but come on. We'll look, and then straight to school."

"Promise," I assured her.

Not ten minutes later, we sat before the empty wedding chest amidst the piles of wedding mementos we'd unearthed from its belly. Mom had even carefully pulled the seams along one edge of the chest's quilted lining so we could peek underneath to check for the recipe. But we'd found nothing except some musty mothballs.

"Hey, you know what? It's all right." Mom squeezed my shoulder. "I think if GG Hazel had wanted anybody to find her recipe, she would've left it in a more practical spot."

"I'm not giving up." I got to my feet. "Julip's looking for the recipe. What happens if she finds it before we do?"

"She'll give it to me," Mom said firmly.

"Mom . . ." I sighed, knowing she was liable to launch into a lecture if I told her again how little I trusted Julip.

"Maybe GG Hazel got rid of the recipe entirely," Mom said, thinking out loud. "She thought it had served its purpose. That people didn't need it anymore."

"I don't buy that for a second." I shouldered my backpack.

"No." Mom's voice was decisive. "I don't either. Not with GG Hazel." Mom began putting albums and wedding cards back into the chest. "Because . . . is there ever really a time when people aren't in need of healing?"

We looked at each other, both thinking about the customers who came into the shop, suffering from loneliness, grief, heartbreak. *Is there ever really a time when people aren't in need of healing? No. No, there isn't.*

That thought was still on my mind when I got to school, right in time for lunch.

Bree grabbed me in a hug before I could sit down at our table, nearly making me drop my tray. "Dace, omigod, we were so worried! You quit texting us with updates on Ginger! How is she? Is she—"

"She's fine." I smiled as Bree collapsed onto the bench in relief.

"Great!" Zari opened her tablet and began typing. "Now I can publish my piece about you and your dad's superb lifesaving skills."

"Actually." The color rose in my cheeks. "We shouldn't get all the credit. Chayton helped out, too."

My eyes skimmed the cafeteria until they found Chayton, sitting with JC and Tad. They were laughing over some joke he'd just told them. His gaze flicked to mine, and he smiled.

I raised my hand in a half wave, smiling back. When I turned back to our table, Zari, Bree, and Maria were all staring at me, openmouthed.

"What's this?" Maria gasped. "A change of heart?"

I shrugged, focusing intently on my turkey sandwich. "Just a truce is all."

"So . . . you two *talked*?" Zari raised an eyebrow. "Got along? Without arguing?"

"Only this morning, but . . . yeah, we got along." It surprised me to say it. It was one thing that I'd decided to make peace with Chayton, but another to realize I'd enjoyed talking with him.

"So you're friends," Bree concluded.

I hesitated. Even if my own stubbornness was preventing me from admitting it just yet, I wanted us to be friends. He'd spent all night taking care of Ginger and done it knowing full well that I might still loathe him come morning. Not just anybody would've done that. Regardless of all the times he'd irked me when we were kids, what he'd done last night said something about who he was now. Something good. "We're . . . working on it," I said slowly.

"Thank goodness," Zari blurted. "If he'd stayed your sworn enemy, we might have had to boycott the Main Street makeover and then I would've missed out on the story."

My heart thumped in my chest, and I knew it was time to tell them. "Actually, today *I* have a story," I said breathlessly. "And it's bigger news than the makeover."

Three pairs of eyes glued to my face. They knew me so well. If I said big news, it meant legit BIG news. I leaned forward, and, in a cascade of whispered words, poured out the story of what Julip had discovered at the library.

"*Dios mío,*" Maria said. That's how I knew she was truly shocked, because she'd shifted into Spanish without even realizing it, something she never did. "So it's really out there somewhere?"

I nodded.

Zari slapped her hands down on the table and stood up. "We've got to check out that tree," she announced, way too loudly.

"*Shhh,*" I whispered, yanking her back into her seat. "I know, but we can't go now. And Julip's probably going to be scoping it out, too."

"We have to stop her." Bree's sweet voice had an edge of panic. "She can't get to it first. What can we do? We have to do something! We have to—"

"Easy there." Maria patted Bree's back consolingly. "We can't do something right this instant."

"No . . ." Zari had a thoughtful, scheming look on her face. "But we *can* keep Julip extremely busy until we have a chance to check out the tree." She pulled out her phone and began typing away. "I'm going to set up an interview with her for after school today, and then we're all going to keep her distracted until—"

"The picnic!" Bree said. "Principal Sawyer made an announcement about it this morning. He said The Panhandle Pickers are performing." She grinned. Bree was a die-hard country music fan, and The Pickers were her favorite band. "Anyway, we can check out the tree during the picnic on Saturday."

I nodded. "And maybe we can throw Julip off the trail until then."

"There are lots of hearts in Bonnet," Maria said. "There's the heart in the stained glass window at Bonnet Baptist . . ."

"And the heart on the water tower," Bree added.

"Weren't the stools inside the Bonnet Soda Shop heart-shaped?" I asked. We all nodded, letting the possibilities for hiding places sink into our buzzing brains. "We'll make a list of every heart in town where the recipe could be hidden. We'll check them out, one at a time, and if we don't find the recipe . . ."

"We'll drop a hint to Julip. A red herring, to lead her in the wrong direction." Zari rubbed her hands together. "I *love* it. It screams investigative reporting tactics."

"We'll get started after school," I said determinedly. "If that recipe still exists, we're going to find it."

Chapter Six

I rubbed a small circle in the dusty window of the Bonnet Soda Shop, then peeked out through it.

A dozen Bonneters were working on Main Street, even though the Saturday makeover wouldn't officially kick off for another hour. I picked out Julip right away, colorful in her bubble-gum pink dress.

Zari stuck her face beside mine and whispered, "Only Julip could make manual labor look so fashionable." She giggled. "Can you hear that? She's already giving orders."

"No no no no no." Julip's honeyed Southern drawl had become a tightrope of commands. "I asked for red geraniums to be hung from each lamppost, not pink geraniums to be hung from each awning. People. Get it together."

I swung away from the window. "We have to hurry," I told my friends. "Julip's down at the other end of the street right now, but she'll be close soon enough."

Bree and Maria were busy lifting the musty, grayed tarp off the soda shop's counter and chairs. A cloud of dust rose in the air, making me cough, but I waved it away impatiently, moving to the row of pink heart-shaped swivel chairs.

Bree sighed. "Aw, I miss this place. The root beer floats were my favorite."

"Never mind that now," Maria said. "Start searching."

We moved from chair to chair, inspecting each one carefully. They were bolted to the floor and still surprisingly sturdy, and all we discovered was some stale, cement-like gum stuck to their undersides. When we reached the last chair, though, the seat wobbled.

"This one's loose." I wiggled the cushion a bit more and it came away in my hands. I turned it over and my breath hitched as I spotted the word "heartstring" written on the underside of the cushion. *Could this be it?*

With a racing pulse, I tilted the seat toward the dim light from the window, trying to make out the rest of the faint, messy writing.

"What does it say?" Bree squeaked. "Is it the recipe?"

"'My . . . heartstring,'" I read slowly, "'is forever . . . tied to yours.'" I looked up into my friends' expectant faces. "My heartstring is forever tied to yours."

Bree clasped her hands to her chest. "Awwww." She smiled. "It's a love note."

"Sweet. But *not* what we're looking for," Maria said flatly.

I felt a mixture of disappointment and curiosity. Whoever had written this note had to have at least known about Heartstring Pie. "I wonder who—"

"Who did what?" The voice was so loud in the quiet room that we all shrieked, and I dropped the seat top to the floor, where it landed with a deafening clatter.

"Chayton!" I yelled in both relief and exasperation when

I saw him standing in the doorway. "You scared the beans out of us!"

"What?" he asked, his expression playful. "Did you think I was GG Hazel's ghost, come back to claim her recipe?"

"Wait . . ." My eyes narrowed. "How did you know—"

"You all are about as subtle as a bull dancing the cancan." He laughed. "You were snooping under the rosebushes at Bonnet Baptist on Wednesday afternoon, then looking under the heart bench in front of Vino's Pizzeria Thursday. But I really knew something was up when I saw you climb the water tower yesterday."

"You've been spying on us?" I folded my arms.

He held up his hands. "Not me. My mom. She's been sneaking around, checking every place you've looked all week."

"Red herrings." Zari nodded proudly.

"Anyway, it wasn't hard to put two and two together," Chayton said.

I rolled my eyes. *Great.* We'd been found out. "So what do you know?" I demanded.

"I know about Hazel's last words, and that my mom, and apparently all of you, think they're a clue to finding the pie recipe. Mom's been talking about it all week." When I frowned, he laughed. "Don't worry, Dace. I'm not here to sabotage your search. I came to help. Mom's walking this way right now, and she has no place finding that recipe before you do. It belongs to your family."

"That is *so* sweet," Bree whisper-crooned, and Maria smacked her arm.

"Anyway, I told her I'd start looking," Chayton continued. "You guys go outside and get started with the makeover. If I find anything else in here, I'll keep it safe until I can get it to you. Okay?"

I hesitated, the question of whether or not to trust Chayton looming over me. Zari gave a small nod, as if to say, *Too late not to.* And if I couldn't trust him, how could I ever have Chayton as my friend? I sucked in a breath, then said, "Okay. Thanks."

We smiled at each other, and then Chayton walked toward me. "I'll put this back." His fingers grazed mine as he took the seat cushion I was holding. My skin tingled at his touch. "I'm pretty sure these words weren't meant for my mom anyway."

Then Zari was tugging my arm, leading me out of the shop alongside Maria and Bree.

"We are live in less than five minutes," Julip announced through the bullhorn. "Paintbrushes should be in every hand."

"She seems annoyed," I whispered to Zari as we stood together on the Pies N' Prattle porch. We were in the positions assigned to us by the *Prairie Living* camera crew.

Zari nodded. "Because she didn't find the recipe in the soda shop."

My friends and I had watched tensely from a distance as Julip had disappeared into the soda shop two minutes after we left it. When she and Chayton came out again, Chayton gave us a discreet thumbs-up, so I knew she hadn't found anything. It was a relief, but that didn't mean we could stop looking.

"Do you think she's choreographed a synchronized brush-stroke for us?" I asked Zari now.

She stifled a giggle in her elbow, since her hands were holding a brush and an open paint can. "I wouldn't put it past her. Look at Bree and Maria."

Bree and Maria had been assigned a post across the street from us at The Whole Enchilada, and they were hanging colorful lanterns outside the restaurant while posing for some test shots for the cameras. I could see Bree's unnaturally wide smile and Maria's shaking fingers. They weren't the only ones flustered, either. Over the last half hour, most of the population of Bonnet had shown up for the makeover, bubbling with eagerness. But Julip was a bulldozer and she'd shoveled instructions over everyone about what to wear today, down to hair accessories, shoes, and belt buckles.

As a result, folks I'd only ever seen wearing denim had shown up in full flower-print skirts and kitten heels. What was absurd was that Julip was expecting them to paint and hammer in these outfits straight out of Perfectville. We'd also been instructed to smile as much as possible, and to look extremely busy and conversational. I'd never realized how much of a ruse reality TV was, and I didn't like it.

This wasn't the Bonnet that I knew and loved; it was a fabricated utopia. I was just about to say so to Zari when I caught sight of Chayton walking toward us with Caroleen beside him. Caroleen was smiling at him like he was the best view in Bonnet. He whispered something to her, and she threw back her head, laughing.

I felt an unfamiliar and unpleasant twinge in my chest. But a moment later, it was gone, replaced with a surge of adrenaline as Chayton left Caroleen to join me on the porch with his own paint can and brush.

"Is this spot taken?" He nodded toward a section of peeling white paint under the Pies N' Prattle bay window. He rolled his shirtsleeves and tied back his black locks into a low ponytail.

For a second, I wondered if his hair was as soft as it looked. My heart skipped, and I shoved the thought away in confusion. Where had *that* come from?

"Don't get sloppy with that paint, now," I teased. "Use even brushstrokes. Up, down, side to side. And smile pretty for the cameras."

"Sounds like you doubt my skill." Chayton's eyes sparkled.

"The last time I saw you paint was in kindergarten. Remember what you did to Ms. Cassie's walls?"

"Hey, you said you wanted to have a contest to see who could paint the best garden. You can't fit an entire garden on a single sheet of paper." He waved his brush at me. "You were a bad influence."

"Me?" I said. "I just wanted to see if you were up to the challenge."

His laugh was cut short when his mom called his name.

"Chayton," she said again, marching onto the porch. "Has it escaped your notice that there are camera crews lining this main street?"

"There are?" Chayton's jaw dropped in mock shock.

Julip leaned toward him. "This is no laughing matter. You know what this means to me, and . . . didn't I ask you to change? I told you I brought a pair of nicer jeans for you."

Chayton glanced down at his dirt-smudged, faded jeans. "These look more authentic. Like I walked over straight from the stables, which is actually true."

"That was an hour ago. You had plenty of time . . ." Julip pursed her lips. "Why do you have to go out of your way to cause a scene?"

Chayton's smile faded. "I'm not causing a scene, Mom. Don't put me in the show if my jeans are going to screw everything up." He shrugged. "I don't care."

He turned away from her then and focused intently on his painting. Julip opened her mouth to argue, but she was interrupted by a guy from the camera crew. She gave Chayton one more disgruntled glance, then hurried off the porch as a makeup artist applied powder to her face.

"Wow," Zari muttered. I turned to shush her but Chayton hadn't heard. He was slapping paint onto the porch and holding the brush in a death grip.

I'd never seen him so ruffled, and I had the urge to talk to him about it, but I heard Julip Freedell's singsong voice resonating up and down Main Street.

"Hi, y'all, and welcome back to *Prairie Living*." Julip was grinning for one of the cameras. "Because I care about you so much, today I'm sharing something special with you. My hometown of Bonnet, Texas!"

The cameras—there were at least a dozen shooting from different vantage points all over Main Street—were zooming in on smiling faces and waving hands. A producer sat at a laptop looking at all the shots, deciding on the best ones to stream live.

Julip kept on with her monologue, talking about how much she loved Bonnet and what a wonderful childhood she'd had in our bucolic town. As everyone painted, hung up new store signs, and repaired broken shutters and porch railings, Julip moved among us, giving hugs to her old classmates and chatting with everyone as if we were her long-lost best friends.

At one point, Julip had a camera follow her inside Pies N' Prattle to share the shop's history. From my post on the porch, I watched Mom beam with pride as she displayed one of her freshly baked peach pies for the camera. Then, much to my horror, she and Julip waved me into the shop, and a camera homed in on me.

"Here she is now," Julip was saying to the cameras, "Dacey Culpepper Biel, Hazel Culpepper's great-granddaughter."

Despite my hammering heart, I mustered a smile for the camera.

"Edie . . ." Julip turned to my mom. "I bet you're tickled pink to have Dacey working in the shop with you."

"Of course I am," Mom said evenly. "I love teaching her the pie business, and I am proud to be carrying on our family's legacy with her beside me. It's my hope that someday, she'll claim her spot in the long line of Culpepper master bakers."

My insides knotted and my skin turned slick.

"Well, Dacey," Julip said to me. "If there was one pie you'd bake for our audience right now, what would it be?"

Panic rose in my throat. I stared into the camera lens and it stared back like an enormous black eye, seeing past my twitching smile to my innermost secrets. *It knows*, I thought. *It knows I can't bake.*

"Heartstring Pie!" I blurted, then realized with horror that I'd just said I would bake a pie that no longer existed.

Julip, though, looked positively beside herself with delight. "Of course you would!" She faced a camera full-on. "A true Culpepper through and through." Then she winked at me. "If anyone can find your great-gran's long-lost recipe, it's you."

Julip turned back to my mom to sample a bite of the peach pie, and the cameraman motioned that it was safe for me to leave. I took a step, then had to steady myself against the doorway.

A master baker, Mom had said. And she'd said it with such pride, as if I could make all of her dreams for the shop come true.

Only . . . I couldn't.

I walked back to the porch and picked up my paintbrush. The Main Street makeover was working. Geraniums hung cheerfully in baskets from freshly painted lampposts, and the new coats of paint on storefronts were transforming drab browns and grays to bright creams, whites, and blues. Our Main Street looked more revived and welcoming than it had in years. Except for my corner of the Pies N' Prattle porch, still a faded gray.

I had to finish, but my heart wasn't in it. Not anymore.

"Aren't you going to eat?" Maria asked me as she finished her bowl of gumbo. "You haven't touched your food."

I glanced down at my gumbo, then shook my head, holding it out to her. "Not hungry."

An hour ago, the last string of lights had been strung on Main Street to resounding cheers and applause. Now everyone in Bonnet had come to the Jenkins ranch for the celebratory picnic. While dozens of people helped themselves to the boiled crawfish buffet, others played games of horseshoes or cornhole. And just as Julip had promised, The Panhandle Pickers were tuning their guitars and warming up on the outdoor stage, getting ready to sing. Zari, Bree, and Maria were having a great time, but I was preoccupied. All I could think about was the oak tree, and what we hadn't found underneath it.

Zari sat down beside me with her own pile of crawfish and corn on the cob. She took one look at my face and her brow creased with worry. "I know you're disappointed," she said quietly. "I'm sorry. The tree seemed like a sure bet."

While Julip had been busy finishing filming on Main Street, Chayton had signaled us, and we'd all slipped away to the ranch. There, we'd ridden horses out to the heart-shaped tree and started our search. Zari had held a flashlight for me while I peeked into the knothole in the cradle of the tree's trunk.

"There's definitely something in there," I said breathlessly as I spotted a gleam of gold. After a few minutes gently teasing it from where it was wedged (with the help of tweezers from Chayton's pocketknife), I slid out a heart-shaped medal on a purple ribbon from the knothole.

"It's a purple-heart medal," Chayton said instantly. "The medal given to servicemen for heroic acts in wartime. This one's old."

"World War II old?" I asked, thinking of the soldiers GG Hazel had cared for.

He nodded. "Maybe."

I turned the medal over in my hands. "Your granddad told you the war veterans used to come out here for picnics . . . and Heartstring Pie."

"One of the veterans must have lost it here," Maria suggested.

"No." I stared at the medal, feeling an uncanny certainty. "I think whoever put it here left it on purpose." For a split second, I saw in my mind's eye a young soldier—maybe no older than eighteen—eating a slice of Heartstring Pie, and then, with tears in his eyes, tucking the medal into the tree. "Maybe he left it to remember someone . . ."

"To honor them," Bree said. "Like leaving some of your heart behind."

We all fell silent at that, and then, with as much care as I could, I tucked the medal back into the knothole. "It belongs here," I said, pressing my hand protectively over the knothole.

"We should head back," Chayton said then. "The picnic will start soon."

The ride back had been a quiet one, with each of us lost in our own thoughts. It wasn't even the disappointment of not finding the recipe, but the weight of what we'd found, that made us all subdued.

"It's not that we didn't find the recipe," I said to Zari now as she buttered her corn. "For the first time, I realize what GG Hazel did, the people she helped. They're not just stories anymore. They're *real*."

"I know," Zari said.

"It's a big responsibility is all." I sighed, and Zari squeezed my hand.

"I believe in you," she said. "We all do. If the recipe exists, you're the one who'll find it."

I smiled. "Thanks." Then, because I sensed that if I didn't do something to snap out of my funk, I was going to drag my friends down with me, I gave Bree a feigned look of horror. "How many of those crustaceans have you eaten?"

"That's thirty and counting," Bree said proudly as she dropped another crawfish shell onto the growing pile on her plate. We all laughed appreciatively.

"I can't believe this spread." Zari gestured to the tables piled high with crawfish, corn, watermelon, shrimp gumbo, and biscuits and gravy. "And I heard Mrs. Beaumont say that it's all Julip's *Prairie Living* recipes."

My eyes, against my will, swept the party for Chayton. I hadn't seen him since we'd gotten back to the stables.

Maria spotted him before I did. "Look who nabbed the first dance with Chayton."

Caroleen and Chayton were on the dance floor, performing a showstopping two-step while the *Prairie Living* camera crew filmed them. Julip was looking on in obvious delight, and I understood why. Moving seamlessly, with their bright smiles, Chayton and Caroleen made a picture-perfect couple. *Prairie Living* fans were going to gobble it up.

I swallowed, feeling like something was lodged in my throat. What was it? Jealousy? That wasn't possible . . . was it? But I'd felt it earlier when I'd seen them together on Main Street, too.

"Hey." Zari nudged me. "You know how Caroleen flirts. It doesn't mean anything."

"I know! What do I care anyway?" It came out too defensively, and I could tell from the look Zari gave me that she wasn't buying it. I forced myself to look away from the dance floor and gulp down a couple crawfish, which only made that lump in my throat worse.

A couple minutes later, The Panhandle Pickers played the opening chords to "Cold Mountain, Warm Arms," and Bree squealed. It was her favorite song. She grabbed Maria's hand. "Come on! Let's dance."

Every kid in Bonnet had learned the Texas two-step before we'd learned how to read and write. So within seconds, Maria and Bree had dragged Tad and JC onto the dance floor with them, and soon, a bunch of other kids followed suit.

Zari nudged me. "Dace . . . look out. Better put on your dancing shoes."

"Wha—?" My voice caught as I glanced up to see Chayton holding out his hand to me. Sunlight glinted in his bottomless brown eyes, and they struck me as daring and gentle all at once.

"Come on, enemy mine." He grinned. "Let's show them how it's done."

I hesitated, thinking about how perfect he'd looked out there earlier with Caroleen. "Nah. I'm sure you can find plenty of other partners."

"Hey, I'm standing here, aren't I?" He extended his hand farther toward me. "I know you can ride a horse. Let's see if you can dance."

I laughed, unable to resist the challenge. "Oh, I can dance all right," I countered, sliding my fingers into his. "Just make sure *you* can keep up."

My heart accelerated as we took the floor, and Chayton stepped off into an easy two-stepping glide. He was as confident dancing as he was with everything else. He spun me around, then caught me by the waist, and my face warmed.

"How am I doing so far?" He grinned.

He hadn't spun Caroleen like this, but no way was I going to let on that this made me happy. "All right, I guess," I said nonchalantly. "Only I expected more—"

Before I could finish, he dipped me to the right, then left, swinging my legs with each dip. *Whoa.* The way he'd danced before had been amateur compared to this. He exuded the lighthearted ease that when we were younger I'd found annoying, but right now, I had to admit, was really charming. A few people watching us whooped, and when he set me back onto my feet, I was breathless and laughing.

"Okay, okay," I said. "You can definitely dance."

He gave a single nod of satisfaction. "Why thank you kindly, ma'am," he said with an exaggerated drawl.

The music slowed into a ballad. Chayton drew me in, close enough to feel his breath against my hair. I found myself enjoying the slow dance in companionable silence with him, but then two familiar voices floated from the picnic tables. I glanced over to see Mom and Julip, deep in conversation.

"I don't think you understand what a huge marketing opportunity this could be for you," Julip was saying. "You could say you'd found the Heartstring Recipe, and nobody would know any different. Just . . . make up a new recipe and give it the Heartstring name!"

"I couldn't," Mom said. "It wouldn't be right. Nobody else might know the difference, but *I* would. Besides, I already tried to re-create it once, back when I was a teenager, and the oven caught fire. You may think the curse is hogwash, but I'm not risking my oven again."

"Edie, you're being foolish," Julip said. "You could share the Heartstring recipe with the world. Sell it and your shop would have a real future!"

My face burned as I listened, and I stepped on Chayton's toes in my distraction.

"Sell it? I could never," Mom said. "GG Hazel didn't sell her Heartstring Pie. She gave it away to folks who needed it. Even if I found the recipe, I wouldn't sell it for a profit. Our recipes are family secrets and will stay that way. If people want a taste of Culpepper pie, they'll have to come to Bonnet to get it."

Julip frowned. "At least consider sharing some of your other recipes, then. I could help you publish them in a book. With the *Prairie Living* brand on it, a book like that would sell—"

"Oooof!" I stumbled, falling forward into Chayton's arms.

"Whoa." Chayton laughed. "*Now* who's got two left feet?" He lifted my chin with his finger so he could see my face, and his smile faded into concern. "Hey, what's the matter?"

I shook my head. Julip's persistent profit-making schemes were unbelievable. More than that, though, I felt guilty. Every decision Mom made about Pies N' Prattle carried so much weight, and now I knew she wasn't just making those decisions for her, or GG Hazel. She was making them for me, the daughter she envisioned becoming a master baker. It was all too much.

"I-I'm . . ." I desperately tried to think of an excuse to leave. "I haven't checked on Ginger all day. I need to. Now."

It sounded lame, and his narrowing eyes told me that he saw right through my lie.

"Dace, I heard my mom talking just now, too. Don't let her get to you—"

I stepped out of Chayton's arms so suddenly that I bumped into Zari, who was waltzing by with Dante. She shot me a quizzical look but I waved a hand at her.

"It's not that," I lied to Chayton. "I just need a break from this." I backed off the dance floor. "All of this."

He started toward me. "I'll come with you to the stables—"

"No!" It came out harsher than I intended, and he looked surprised and a little hurt. My heart panged. "No, it's all right," I said, more softly. "I'm sure your mom wants you to stay."

I ran for the stables, straight to the sanctuary of Ginger's stall. I saddled her quickly, then slipped out the front entrance to avoid the picnic-goers. I suspected that if Chayton saw me riding, he'd want to follow, but right now, I needed to be alone with Ginger, to gallop her through the wide eastern meadow, and to forget all about Pies N' Prattle for a little while.

Chapter Seven

The next morning, I woke to the familiar sound of Mom's slippered feet padding toward my bedroom.

She opened my door a crack. "Pies N' Prattle wake-up call. You in?"

I pulled the covers over my head. "Not today, Mom. Too tired." I made my voice sound drowsy, even though I'd been lying awake for an hour, too consumed with my thoughts to sleep.

"Okay, Too Tired, you're off the hook." It came out light-hearted, but there was a tinge of surprise in her tone. I knew how much Mom enjoyed my company in the kitchen. She did the baking while I unloaded the industrial dishwasher and started brewing coffee and iced tea, getting the shop ready for opening. "I'll give you two hours, but I need you at the shop by seven thirty so I can deliver some blueberry crepe pies to Bonnet Baptist for their coffee hour."

"Kay," I mumbled. A second later, my door clicked closed. I sighed, guilt and relief a bitter blend in my stomach. Then I grabbed my phone, reading the worried texts Zari, Bree, and Maria had all sent me last night after I'd left the picnic. I loved the three of them for their caring, and I texted back to assure them I was okay.

A few minutes after I heard Mom's car pull out of the driveway, Dad flung open my door.

"I made you a café au lait," he said matter-of-factly. "Father/daughter confab. My office. Five minutes."

Being around animals so much must have given my dad some sort of weird extrasensory abilities, like how dogs and cats know when earthquakes are coming. I got up and dressed, then met him in his office.

He handed me the coffee—a special treat he made for me that Mom pretended to be annoyed by, even though she really didn't mind too much.

"Want to talk about it?" he asked.

I shrugged, sinking down into one of the chairs. "What?"

Dad took a long swig of his coffee. "You didn't want to go to the shop this morning, for one. And two, you disappeared from the picnic hours before it ended *and* before I got to do the Chicken Dance with you."

I laughed. "Missing the Chicken Dance was premeditated."

"Ouch." Dad clutched his chest, making me laugh harder. "Seriously, though. We're worried about you. You haven't seemed like yourself for the last few weeks."

I stared into the white foaminess of my café au lait. "I've been thinking a lot about the shop. And GG Hazel. That's all." I swallowed, unable to say more. I was too afraid to tell him the entire truth.

"Hey." Dad crouched down in front of my seat so I'd have to look him in the eye. "If you're worried about the shop closing, don't." His tone was gentle, consoling. "I shouldn't have even hinted that it was in trouble. Mom and I know how much you love it, and we're doing everything in our power to save it."

I practically winced at his words. Dad—who usually got me so well—had missed the mark entirely. I couldn't tell him that, though, because then I'd have to tell him what I was *really* worried about. He'd be disappointed, and Mom—Mom would be devastated.

"Thanks, Dad. I know you are," I said quickly. I pecked his cheek, then stood, gulping down the rest of my café au lait so quickly I barely tasted it. "I think I'll head to the shop now."

His forehead crinkled. "Are you sure? We have time for rummy before you go."

"After dinner tonight, I promise." I turned to the door, then hesitated. "Thanks for the talk, Dad. It helped."

It was the teensiest fib, and one that was made worth it when Dad's face lit up with the satisfaction of a successful parenting moment. "I'm glad, Honeybee. I'm here to help anytime."

"I know." And I did. Only this time, he couldn't help.

I dragged my feet getting to Pies N' Prattle, unable to shake my funk. But when I stepped inside the shop and saw Chayton behind the counter, tying one of Mom's gingham aprons around his middle, I was so surprised, I couldn't help laughing.

"Trying out a new fashion trend for *Prairie Living*?" I asked.

He grinned. "Of course. What do you think?"

"Cute. But you need to accessorize." I dug a rolling pin out from under the counter and put it in his hand, then stepped back, appraising. "Not bad. The ruffles work in your favor."

"Course they do." He winked. "When you look as good as me, everything works in your favor." He flexed his bicep.

I rolled my eyes. "You're impossible."

"Definitely. It's why you like me."

Before I could get flustered by that, Mom swung through the kitchen door.

"Dacey! Oh good!" She tossed me an apron. "I was about to teach Chayton how to bake an apple pie, but I've got to get these pies wrapped up for Bonnet Baptist . . ." She disappeared into the kitchen again, clearly in a hurry.

I looked at Chayton skeptically. "You want to learn how to bake a pie?"

"Oh, absolutely," he said. "I feel called to, in fact. It's what I've been missing my whole life."

I narrowed my eyes at him. "Does this have something to do with your mom?"

I could tell from his overly executed shrug that it did. Before I could press him, Mom rushed in from the kitchen with boxes of pies, and we went out to help her load them into the car.

"I hope Mr. Victor's been keeping an eye on Tootsie," Mom muttered as she opened her car door. "Yesterday I nearly ran off the road trying to avoid that pig. She spends more time on the loose than she does in her pen!"

"If she's blocking the road, just offer her some pie," Chayton suggested.

"No pig is going to eat *my* pie. Oh no!" Mom slapped her forehead. "Chayton! I almost forgot about your baking lesson."

She glanced at me. "Dacey, you can show Chayton how it's done. Go on and get started."

My heart pounded. Had Mom completely lost her senses? "Mom, I can't—"

Mom turned the key in the ignition. "Course you can, Dace. Otherwise Chayton'll be waiting around all day. I'll be back before the shop opens." Then she pulled away from the curb.

I gulped, dread climbing my insides. When I turned to Chayton, he was smiling expectantly.

"So?" he asked, following me back into the shop. "Where do we start?"

"You don't really want to be here." It came out abruptly, hostile even. I could tell by the surprise in his eyes.

"Sure I do."

I shook my head. "You're here because of your mom. Right?"

He played with the rolling pin on the counter. "Okay. Confession time. So . . . yeah. Mom wanted me to come over. She was hoping your mom would teach me how to make one of the Culpepper pie recipes and then—"

"She'd share it on *Prairie Living*?" I asked incredulously.

Chayton nodded, looking way calmer than I would've expected him to.

"Unbelievable," I hissed. "Your mom thought—what?—that she could trick us into giving up one of the family recipes?"

Chayton held up his hands. "It's scummy, I know." All trace of jokester Chayton was gone. There was a heaviness to his expression—a sadness that usually he tried to disguise with laughter. "Look. My mom is . . . difficult. She's always been caught up in her show, and she gets so obsessed with its success that she forgets what's right and wrong."

"And you go along with it." It was an accusation, and not one that came out gently.

"No!" he said. "Not at all. I hate that she's like that." His eyes darkened. "I hate that I've spent the last two years getting dragged all over Texas so she could film her show. Most of the time I wasn't even in a real school. I had tutors. And my dad's not in the picture at all. Hasn't been since I was a baby." He ran a hand through his hair. "It's *not* like I blame my mom. It's just that, up until we came back here, she's all I've had."

I thought about Chayton traveling all over Texas, not having much of a dad. It was so different from having parents like mine, who could finish each other's sentences and had always been there for me.

I looked down, feeling some of my defensiveness dissipating. "I'm sorry. That must be hard."

"Yeah," Chayton said. "Well. It's been nice staying with Granddad and Granny. Being with them feels good. Like a legit home. And I love helping out on the ranch."

I nodded, but a lingering doubt nagged at me. "But . . . if you don't agree with your mom then . . . why did you come here today?"

"Partly to get her off my case. She could nag the ear off a donkey." He gave a short laugh. "And partly because Caroleen asked me to go see that new movie *Lost Without You*."

My heart dipped to my toes. "She did?" I tried to make my voice airy, as if I didn't care, but it came out sharply pitched.

He shrugged. "Tad keeps telling me she has a thing for me—"

"Caroleen has a thing for every boy," I blurted, then blushed.

"You don't sound happy about it." A slow smile spread across his face. "Her liking me."

"Wha—no! I don't care." Only my burning face betrayed that I did. I fixed my messy bun. "So . . . why didn't you? Go with Caroleen to the movie, I mean?"

"Not what I'm into these days," he said offhandedly, but his smile had grown as he watched me. "I like movies that are more challenging." My pulse spiked. Why did it feel like he might not be talking about movies at all? "Anyway, there was another reason I came here today." He paused. "To see you. I was worried after you left the picnic yesterday. You seemed upset, and I wanted to make sure you were okay." His eyes found mine and lingered until I broke his gaze. "Are you? Okay?"

I hardly knew anymore, especially once I realized that I liked the fact that he cared. Really liked it. "I'm fine." I ducked into the kitchen to hide my blush, and he followed.

"And by the way, I *wasn't* going to share any of the Culpepper recipes with my mom," he said solemnly. "You have to know that."

The thumping of my heart answered before I did. "I do," I said. "And Mom wouldn't have taught you how to bake one of the *Culpepper* pies anyway. Those are for my eyes only." I checked the clock and turned toward the coffeemaker. "I better start getting ready for the open."

He blinked. "Hang on. What about my pie lesson? Your mom promised."

My dread returned full force. I wanted to tell him the truth— that I couldn't teach him how to bake a pie because I couldn't bake a decent pie myself, but the words wouldn't come. My stubbornness and pride got the better of me. Chayton had never seen me fail at anything. We'd always equaled each other as rivals, and I didn't want to admit to sucking at what I was supposed to be the best at.

Maybe this time would be different. Maybe I'd get it right. Besides, I didn't want him to leave. That was the bigger reason for what I said next.

"Okay," I relinquished. "One basic apple pie coming up."

He smiled. "Bet I can roll a better pie crust than you."

I smiled even as my stomach dove to my toes. What I thought was, *Oh, you can roll a better crust. No doubt about it.* What I said was, "Bring it on."

Chapter Eight

"Okay, that's the last of the Granny Smiths," Chayton said, adding the handful of apple slices to the mixing bowl.

"Great." I tried to tamp down the nervousness in my voice. "Now measure out the cinnamon and sugar and stir it into the apples."

"On it." He sprinkled a small pile of cinnamon into his palm.

"You'll want to use the teaspoons and measuring cups," I said.

"Where's the fun in that?" He dumped the cinnamon into the bowl. I watched with stirrings of jealousy as he eyeballed the amount of sugar as well, pouring it directly into the mixing bowl from the bag of sugar. "I can't mess up apples too badly, right? They're delicious no matter what."

I didn't say a word, but instead focused on adding the flour to the industrial mixer. Of course I'd measured the flour, sugar, salt, and ice-cold butter *exactly*, too afraid of mistakes to improvise. I watched as the paddle spun in the mixture, churning the flour and butter into bigger and bigger clumps until at last it became a lump of dough.

Phew. So far, so good. I carefully lifted the dough and, after sprinkling it with some cold water, kneaded it into a ball.

"What happens now?" Chayton moved to stand beside me. Our shoulders brushed, and warmth rushed over me. Being in the kitchen with him was nerve-wracking, and it wasn't just because I was trying so hard not to fail at this pie. I was hyper-attuned to his every movement, and caught myself sneaking glances at him when I didn't think he'd notice.

When I'd first seen him again after all those years apart, I'd been struck by how cute he was. Only, now his cuteness seemed to be growing with every passing second, as if the moment I'd let go of my old grudge against him, the curtain had been lifted from my eyes. He'd been humming to himself as we worked, seeming to enjoy even the mundane task of peeling and slicing apples.

"Now we freeze the dough for fifteen minutes," I said, "and then we roll it out and press it into the pie pan."

We wrapped the dough in cling wrap and put it in the freezer. Then we set out the pies Mom had already baked in the glass display in the main room and made sure the napkin dispensers and sugar and creamer containers were full. As we worked, we talked about school and the ranch, about how much Chayton enjoyed working with his granddad and how much I loved helping my dad with his vet visits. Our conversation was comfortable and quick-flowing, and even though my mind kept returning to the pie I knew we'd have to finish making, somehow being with Chayton made me feel more at ease.

When the timer buzzed to signal that the dough was ready, we both startled—that's how absorbed in our conversation we'd been.

I brought the chilled dough from the freezer into the main room, setting it on the counter. Chayton clapped his hands. "Okay. I'm ready to roll."

"Be my guest," I said, relieved that he wanted to try this part, since dough always seemed to prove my greatest adversary. I sprinkled some flour on the rolling pin before handing it to him. "You have to roll pretty quickly, because if the dough gets too soft it will start to stick to the pin and the counter."

He held up the rolling pin in one hand as if he were getting ready to perform a magic trick. "Watch and be amazed!"

I held my breath as he brought the rolling pin down. The moment he pressed into the dough, it crumbled into a hundred pieces.

Oh no.

"Ladies and gentlemen, don't be alarmed. None of the dough used in this trick has been harmed in any way . . ." He was grinning and scooping the dough up in his hand, trying to press it back together.

"That's . . . not what's supposed to happen." I tried to re-form a ball of dough, sprinkling a little water on it, but every time I pressed the dough between my fingertips, it crumbled more and more. My temples pricked with perspiration as frustration rose in my chest. "I can't believe this. I did exactly what I was supposed to do—"

"Obviously this is nonconformist dough." Chayton's voice was light. "It's rebelling—"

"Stop!" My yell startled Chayton out of his joking. "It's not funny!"

His eyes widened in surprise. "It's a *little* funny—"

"No it's not!" The furnace inside me exploded from my mouth. "I'm. So. Sick. Of. This!" I grabbed the rolling pin, shaking it. "No matter how many times I try, I can't ever get it right!"

My fury was a tsunami, sweeping logic away. I didn't feel the rolling pin leave my hand. I didn't even see it fly across the room or hit the wall.

I heard the crash, though. The sound of the glass shattering made me jump. What followed was an eerie silence as Chayton and I leaned over the counter to stare at the splintered picture frame on the floor. The faded newspaper photo of GG Hazel stared up at us through shards of glass.

It might've been a trick of the light, but I swear, in that moment, my great-grandmother looked straight at me, her face crushed with disappointment.

I was heaving breaths, my face hot.

Chayton whistled. "Well. At least you weren't aiming for *me* this time." His voice was playful, and absolutely maddening.

I whirled on him, clutching the countertop, not trusting myself to let go in case I had the urge to throw something else. "If you hadn't come here asking to make pie, none of this would've happened."

"But Dace, you love bak—"

"I'm horrible at baking!" I shouted. "I can't make pie. At! All!" I grabbed a second wad of dough from the counter, strangling it in my fist. "I screw up every single time. Everyone says I'll grow into my talent." I pummeled the dough into the counter. "The only thing I'm growing is my aim—"

My breath hitched as Chayton caught my hands, pulling them gently from the dough. "Hey." His voice was soft. "Hey, it's okay. Breathe." Still holding my hands, he eased me down to sit on the floor, then joined me there. "Just breathe."

Normally, if it were Zari or Mom or Dad, I would've balked, storming away to continue fuming. Chayton had a way about him, though, a mellowness that I wanted to share. So . . . I breathed. I breathed until the lit fuse inside me fizzled, then puffed out, until the shop came back into focus, until I could feel the warmth of his hands clasping mine.

"Better?" he asked quietly.

I nodded, releasing a long breath. "Sorry. I didn't mean to unload on you."

He shook his head. "Don't be sorry. If I'd known you hated baking so much, I never would've asked you to help me—"

"I don't hate it. If I hated it, I wouldn't care that I stink at it." A laugh erupted, short and bitter, from my mouth. "I want to love it, and this shop. But I can't. Not really. Not when I feel like I don't belong."

Chayton's eyebrows crinkled. "Of course you belong. Your great-grandma, grandma, your mom . . . you. You're all part of the history of the shop."

"Except *they* could all bake." I leaned against the display cabinet. "And not just bake. They all had this . . . way of talking to people, of looking into their hearts and seeing what they needed, what sort of pie would be right for them. They all had this gift . . . that I'm missing."

Chayton didn't say anything, and I began to worry that what I'd said sounded crazy. Then he reached over our heads, retrieving what was left of the pie dough from the countertop. He pinched a piece of dough from the ball and popped it into his mouth.

"Mmmmm. That's *some* delicious pie dough." He took another taste. "Mmmmm. *This* could be your Culpepper gift. This right here."

"Stop it," I said, but I was fighting the urge to laugh and he knew it.

He grinned. "You could totally sell this. Put a big sticker on it that says 'No Baking Required.'"

The laugh I'd been holding in popped out. "So instead of helping Bonnet, I give the town salmonella? Perfect." I pinched a piece of dough for myself. "It is good," I admitted around my mouthful.

"Told ya." He nudged my shoulder. Then the laughter in his eyes turned serious. "Dace, don't give up. If it's important to you, keep trying. You may not think you have what it takes, but I *know* you do."

I scoffed. "You can't know—"

"The night when Ginger was sick," he interjected. "You walked her for hours. You were relentless. Dauntless." He locked eyes on mine. "Someone to be reckoned with."

My heart skipped. I'd never thought of myself in those terms, but the way Chayton described me . . . made me almost believe it could be true.

"You don't have to say that," I said quietly, staring at the floor.

"I wouldn't if I didn't think it was true." He lowered his head so that I'd have to look at him. "Aside from the fact that you're more fun to argue with than anyone else I know, it's what I like best about you."

"Come on." I rolled my eyes. "I drive you crazy."

He grinned. "Occasionally." His face was inches from mine, and suddenly, I couldn't stop staring at his lips. They were so full, so soft-looking. "Dace, are you seriously going to tell me that you haven't figured it out yet? Why I always read the same books as you did when we were kids? Why I entered all those spelling bees?"

He leaned toward me. I swallowed, my pulse hammering. This wasn't the way archrivals behaved around each other. But I wasn't pulling away. I was moving closer. My eyes were closing. *What* was happening?

I heard his voice in my ear, whispering, "It was for you—"

"Dacey, are you here?" Zari's voice jerked me from whatever strange spell I'd fallen under, and Chayton and I both jumped, clunking heads in our surprise.

"Ow!" we howled simultaneously, grabbing our hurting foreheads.

Zari was peeking over the top of the display counter, mouth agape, as she took in the scene. "Sorry," she whispered gleefully. "I didn't know you guys were—"

"We weren't," I said before she could finish. I had a sudden vision of Zari's headline for tomorrow's Bonnet Buzz column. She'd think up something clever, like RIVAL ROMANCE, and Chayton and I would be the subject of school gossip for days.

I stood up so quickly I narrowly missed clunking heads with Chayton again. "Chayton was just about to leave," I said, a little too abruptly.

"I was?" Chayton looked momentarily confused, but then quickly covered it with a smile, seeming to realize our "moment" had passed. "Yup. That's just what I was about to do." He turned for the door, then glanced back at me. "Can I call you later?"

A blush swept my cheeks, and I could feel Zari homing in on it like a bee drawn to honey.

"Sure." I gave him a smile that, though small, I hoped was encouraging.

He smiled back, and then he was gone.

"Da-*cey*!" Zari shrieked. "What was that?" She squeezed my hand. "Was that a before-kiss or after-kiss moment? And if it was an after-kiss moment, I want to hear about the kiss. A. S. A. P." She snapped her fingers to emphasize each letter.

"It was nothing." I grabbed a broom and dustpan from our storage closet. "I've got to clean this up." I gestured to the pieces of the broken picture frame. "I sort of had a meltdown before," I admitted, hoping that would get us off the topic of Chayton.

I was still reeling from our moment together, confused and giddy. His hand in mine, the connection we'd shared—all of that felt as natural as my rivalry with him had before. But how could that be? How could it be so easy for my emotions to switch loyalties? Suddenly, a thought struck me. Maybe my feelings hadn't changed at all. Maybe, on some level, underneath all the competitiveness, I'd always felt pulled to him. Maybe it was the fact that we were drawn to each other that had made us fight.

I shook my head, trying to arrange my unruly thoughts into some form of clarity. It was no use. I needed more time.

It took one glance at Zari, hands on her hips and that insistent look in her eyes, for me to know that I would not be getting that time right now.

"I'll help you clean up." Zari brought a trash can over, then knelt down beside me and carefully began throwing away some of the largest pieces of glass. "But don't try to tell me that what I saw was *nothing*. Was *that* why you had a meltdown? Chayton flirted and you freaked?"

I snorted. "It didn't have anything to do with him. I was trying to bake."

"Ooooh. Gotcha."

I swept a pile of glass into the dustpan, then paused, remembering how I'd relaxed when Chayton had taken my hands. "Actually, Chayton helped me calm down."

"Not too many people can say that." When I shot her a warning look, she shrugged. "What? When you go into Hulk mode, it takes a special talent to bring back Bruce." She smiled at me. "Dace," she whispered, "the way you two were looking at each other. That wasn't a frenemy look, or even a friendly look. You two were in orbit!"

I glanced sideways at her and then we both burst into giggles. "I don't even understand what is happening!" I cried. "Everything's changing, or maybe it's turning into the way it was always supposed to be." I squeezed her hand and we broke into a new wave of giggles. "It's so crazy. I mean, I could get so incredibly irritated with him, but now . . ."

"Now you want to . . ." She made exaggerated smooching noises until I smacked her playfully on the arm.

"I'm not sure what I want," I admitted, "but . . . maybe?" We squealed collectively, but then I sobered. "Zari, listen, you have to promise me something." She nodded, and I hurried on before I lost my nerve. "Promise me you won't write about this in the Buzz, okay?"

A frown flickered across her face. "Wha—there's no way I'd write about this. You know that. You, me, Maria, Bree—our crushes fall under the Top Secret Besties Code of Conduct."

I nodded, but she gave me a long look that said she was doubting my faith in her. "You really thought I'd spill the beans about your love life to the whole school?" Her tone was injured.

"No," I said hastily. "It's just . . . you posted about me throwing the pie at Chayton, and, well, sometimes your column can be a little . . . gossipy?" The last word came out softly.

Zari blew out a frustrated breath. "It's just that current events in this place are about as interesting as a fly on a horse's back! I'd love for just one cool thing to happen in Bonnet. Just one!"

"I know." I picked up a splintered piece of the wooden picture frame. "I'm sorry. I shouldn't have said anything." I smiled at her. "I have total trust in you."

She sat back on her heels, nodding in satisfaction. "Good. Cause when you *do* get around to kissing Chayton—"

"*If* I decide to kiss Chayton," I corrected her, "you'll be the first one I tell."

I turned to toss a piece of wood in the trash, then froze. I lifted the piece of frame to eye level. At the corner seam, where the wood had split and been exposed, there was a tiny hole. Peeking out of it was the edge of a rolled-up slip of paper.

"Hey, I think there's something—" I grasped the filmy edge between my fingernails and carefully slid the curled, yellowed paper from its hole.

"A hidden compartment," Zari said, inspecting the hole the paper had come from. "Very cool." She glanced over my shoulder as I unfurled the paper. "What is it?"

Words, in faded, dainty script, were scrawled across the paper. As I read them, my heart slammed into my throat.

"Omigod," I whispered. "I can't believe this."

It couldn't be. It couldn't possibly be . . .

Chapter Nine

My hands trembled, making the filmy paper flutter like a tiny, hopeful moth.

One cup chocolate chips, two cups crumbled Heath bars . . . the ingredients began.

My eyes flicked to the top of the paper, where, in faint lettering, I saw the words: *Heartstring Pie.*

Lightning bolted through my chest and every cell in my body was humming. No . . . it couldn't be. It *was.* I read the paper again, my brain processing ten times slower than my rocketing pulse.

I looked up at Zari's expectant face. "It's GG Hazel's recipe for Heartstring Pie."

Zari's gaped. "Shut. Up."

"Truth." I could barely breathe, and I couldn't stop staring at the recipe, marveling at its buttermilk and egg ingredients. *Of course!* I thought. *How could none of the Culpeppers have ever figured this out?*

GG Hazel had used the basics for Chess pie, one of the most popular and deeply rooted pies in our region. It made perfect sense—a classic Southern pie for boys longing for a taste of home. Chess pie had been around for hundreds of years. Local folklore had it that its name came from an accented version of the word "chest," because it was a pie so sugary it could be stored in a tin-fronted pie chest instead of a refrigerator.

I shook my head in disbelief. "They tried cream cheese, gelatin, tapioca . . . this whole time everyone got the recipe wrong!"

"I bet she did it on purpose," Zari whispered, glancing around the store as if GG Hazel were right there, listening. "Made it tricky so nobody could ever duplicate it."

"But it's not tricky." I laughed. "It's simple!"

"Then it was the curs—"

I slapped a hand over Zari's mouth before she could finish the word. "Don't say it. Or even think it. *Not* today."

She nodded solemnly, understanding that the discovery of this long-lost treasure was no time to be tossing around superstitions, especially when suddenly, a small part of me believed they might be true.

"Omigod," Zari whispered when I lifted my hand. "I can't believe you found it."

My heart surged once more, the honest-to-goodness reality of it sinking in. I grinned. "Me neither. Omigod."

"Omigod," we said in unison, louder this time, and then shrieked, hugging and dancing around. Both of us began talking at once.

"Of course she would've hidden it with her own photo!"

"I always wondered what it would taste like."

"Your mom and dad are going to flip when you tell them!"

Zari's last comment sank in. "Mom," I said. "She'll be able to bake the pie now . . ."

"And people will come from all over just for a taste." Zari finished my thought for me. She grabbed my hand. "Dace, *you* should try baking it."

"Wha—no." The idea made me so panicky that I instantly stuck the recipe into my shorts pocket, worried that Zari might've jinxed everything just by mentioning my baking. I began sweeping up the last of the mess, ignoring Zari's stare.

"Why not?" Zari pressed. "It's your GG Hazel's special recipe. It's not like other pies, so maybe baking it won't be the same, either."

"But screwing it up will be." I lifted GG Hazel's article from the floor and gently pressed out its crinkles. "No. Mom should be the one to bake it. Her Heartstring Pie will be perfect."

Zari looked like she wanted to say more, but then the shop's door opened and in came Mom. She was followed by half of the First Baptist congregation, Mrs. Beaumont and her knitting friends, plus some of Julip Freedell's *Prairie Living* camera crew.

"What's going on?" I asked Mom as the crew began setting up around the shop.

"Julip wanted a few more shots from inside the shop before the fair next Saturday. More 'organic,' she called it." Mom smiled. "It's good news. The more Pies N' Prattle appears in the show, the better for business." She caught sight of GG Hazel's article, out of its frame, and she frowned. "What happened to the picture?"

"My temper," I confessed. "Sorry. I was trying to teach Chayton how to bake a pie, and, well, you can guess the rest."

She gave me a long look, then kissed my forehead. "Scale of one to ten. Pimple to alien invasion."

"Ughhhh," I mumbled, then reluctantly admitted, "one."

Mom nodded. "We'll look for a new frame at home later. No biggie." She focused her attention on the waiting customers. "All right. Let's get busy." With that, she hurried into the kitchen.

Zari shot me a sympathetic glance. "One is a subjective number. Pimples can be *totally* traumatic."

I laughed, then Zari whispered, "What about the recipe?"

I patted my pocket. "I'll show Mom as soon as they're gone." I nodded toward the cameras. I didn't want to risk any family secrets slipping out in front of all these people.

Zari and I busied ourselves with slicing up pies for the customers, but I couldn't stop thinking about the recipe. It had given me a newfound hope. Maybe I didn't need to worry about being a good baker anymore. I'd discovered GG Hazel's Heartstring Pie recipe. Maybe that could be my contribution to the Culpepper legacy. I didn't need to grow into my talent. I had my gift right here on this small and tattered piece of paper.

The camera crew stayed at Pies N' Prattle into the afternoon, until I gave up on having a chance to talk to Mom about the recipe. Realizing I'd have to wait until after the shop closed, I left for the stables. In all the hullabaloo, I hadn't had the chance to ride Ginger yet today.

As I saddled her and rode her down my favorite trail along the Brazos, I kept an eye out for Chayton. I wanted to see him, to see if we could get back the moment we'd lost at the shop. Every time I thought about it, my breath seemed to leave my body.

My ride, though, was a quiet one, and I turned back toward the stables with disappointment. As I passed the ranch office, I heard the voices of Mr. Jenkins and Julip rollercoastering in an argument.

"It's time you thought about what's best for your son." Mr. Jenkins gravelly voice was quiet but stern. "That's all I'm saying. He's taken to Bonnet, and I love having his help on the ranch."

"But you can't expect me to move *here*." Julip's tone was tight and high. "Bonnet is a sorry town. *Prairie Living* would never survive here. The appeal of the show is the travel—"

"Julip. The producer told you himself that this is probably the show's last season—"

"No. He said the ratings needed a boost, that's all." Her voice rose several notches. "I'm working on a way to fix everything—"

"At Chayton's expense?" Mr. Jenkins asked.

"Chayton is *my* son. He got used to moving around before, and he'll get used to it again. That's all there is to it." Julip's words were clipped and final.

I swung Ginger toward the stables just as Julip threw open the door to Mr. Jenkins's office. The frustration pinching her face disappeared the second she saw me, replaced by her TV-worthy smile.

"Dacey, how nice to see you!" She fluttered her hand in my direction. "We got some charming footage of Pies N' Prattle today."

"Thanks, Ms. Freedell." I smiled through gritted teeth.

"Could you do me a favor?" Her smile widened. "Tell your mom I'll be stopping by tomorrow morning? I want to finalize the details for the pie-eating contest with her. Only six days away!" she singsonged. "And maybe you can convince her to share some of those family recipes she's guarding so closely. You're a smart girl." She winked at me, and I cringed inwardly. "I'm sure you have sense enough to know what's best for the survival of Pies N' Prattle."

Heat flashed over my face, and I felt words clogging my throat. Words about how I could never betray my mom like that, and how dare Julip call Bonnet a "sorry town," or dismiss Chayton's happiness? I swallowed the words down, remembering the hopefulness I'd seen in Mom's face earlier, when she'd talked about how *Prairie Living* could help the shop. I wouldn't do anything to risk the shop's future, and right now, that meant being polite to Julip Freedell.

"I'll tell Mom that you'll be by tomorrow," I said as quickly as I could manage.

Then I hurried Ginger away before my real opinions of Julip got the better of me.

I rolled over in bed and checked the clock. Almost midnight. I flipped my pillow to the cool side and pressed my face into it, groaning. I hadn't slept a single minute since I'd turned off my light hours ago.

GG Hazel's recipe was pressed into my hand, its paper so weathered it felt soft against my palm. I'd been hoping to tell Mom about the recipe tonight. But when I'd gotten back from the stables, only Dad was home. As he closed up the vet clinic, he told me that Mom had taken a dozen pies over to the Gonzalez family.

"They're putting their house up for sale," Dad said, "and Selena is beside herself. Mom will probably be there for a while."

"But they can't move!" I cried. "Their family's lived in Bonnet—"

"For as long as the Culpeppers." Dad nodded while he slid the last patient file back into its cabinet. "And the Jenkins and Beaumonts, and half the other folks who've been here for generations and generations. But Dace, their restaurant's closing and they have two little children to support." He shook his head. "There's not enough of a future for them in our tiny town."

I stared at him, shocked by the uncharacteristic pessimism in his words. "Don't say that. It's not true."

Dad placed his hand against my cheek. "I wish it weren't," he said softly. "Thanks to Julip Freedell and her show, your mom's clinging to this idea that the Bonnet Fair will be our saving grace. But . . . I'm afraid it's not going to be enough."

He switched off the light to his exam room, and together we walked through the hallway that connected his clinic to our kitchen. He grabbed his phone and shot me a bolstering smile.

"Come on, let's order takeout and have a rummy tournament. What's your pleasure? Thai, Indian, Cuban?"

I rolled my eyes at our standing joke. Both of us knew that Vino's Pizzeria was the only place in town that delivered. "Large pizza . . ."

"Extra cheese," Dad finished for me

"But I think I'll pass on the rummy tonight," I said. "I have some homework to finish up, so I'll eat a slice in my room when it comes."

"All right," Dad said. As he called Vino's, I escaped to my bedroom with my tumult of thoughts. I was sure Dad was dead wrong about Bonnet, and that once I told Mom about the Heartstring recipe, everything would be all right. The next minute I'd convinced myself that not even the recipe could help our town.

The pressure of being the sole possessor of the recipe weighed on me until I grabbed my phone, ready to snap a pic of it and text it to Mom, just to have the burden lifted from my shoulders. My battery was dead, though, and by the time I plugged my phone in to charge, I was having second thoughts about texting the recipe anyway. My gut told me it was something I needed to share with Mom face-to-face. It was too big—too important—to compress into a flippant OMG GUESS WHAT?!? text. And I *didn't* want GG Hazel coming back to haunt me if some kind of cyber leak occurred with her precious recipe. No, I decided, I had to show Mom the real deal.

When the pizza arrived, I picked at my slice without any appetite or enthusiasm, staring into space while my homework went ignored. Dad eventually came in to say goodnight, but Mom was still at the Gonzalezes'. Dad told me that Mrs. Gonzalez was so exhausted and upset that Mom had offered to take care of Marco's midnight bottle feeding so Mrs. Gonzalez could sleep. That was *so* Mom.

And now, unbeknownst to Mom, with the midnight hour approaching, GG Hazel's recipe still sat in my hand. I didn't want to let it out of my sight. It was both comforting and distressing to hold. It made me feel closer to GG Hazel than ever before, but it also seemed to be waiting for something from me. But what?

I sat up and threw off my covers, and changed back into my shorts and T-shirt. Then I put the recipe in my pocket, scribbled a note to Mom and Dad, and walked outside, heading for Pies N' Prattle.

The shop was dark, the moonlight washing it in a deep indigo. I started straight for the kitchen, conviction burning in my stomach. Maybe GG Hazel *had* intended the recipe for me. And if that was the case, I'd bake Heartstring Pie. Tonight. I'd prove to my great-grandmother and everyone else that I could do it; that I could live up to the Culpepper name.

Halfway to the kitchen, I faltered, panicking. I sank into the nearest armchair and put my head in my hands.

No, I wouldn't bake the pie. I wouldn't even try.

The only thing worse than worrying if I *might* fail would be actually failing. After all that had happened today—the tornado of emotions I was feeling about Chayton, Julip, the Gonzalezes—I couldn't deal with the possibility of more disappointment. Especially the sort that wouldn't just disappoint me, but all the Culpeppers who'd gone before me. No, I wouldn't try. Not tonight. Maybe not ever.

I leaned back in the chair, my gaze settling on the photo of GG Hazel; Mom had temporarily taped it to the wall. GG Hazel's eyes—two dark pinpricks in the night—looked soulful, satisfied, as if she were content with a life well lived.

She'd poured her love and life into Pies N' Prattle and into helping others, and now Mom was doing the same. *What*, I wondered as my eyelids grew heavy, *would be* my *contribution to our family and this shop?*

Chapter Ten

"Daccy? Dacey! It's time . . ."

GG Hazel? I thought groggily.

"Time for what?" I mumbled.

"Time for school."

I opened my eyes, blinking against the bright light streaming through the shop windows. Mom was leaning over me, her hand on my shoulder. "Sweetie, you slept here all night. I didn't see your note until this morning."

I jerked upright in the chair, then put a hand to my neck, trying to work out the crick that had formed as I'd slept. I checked my watch: Seven forty-five. School started in fifteen minutes. "Oh no! I'll be late."

"Nah." Mom smiled, motioning to my outfit. "You're already dressed." She held up my school bag. "*And* I brought your bag with me."

"Thanks." I slung it over my shoulder and twisted my hair into a mussed topknot, then took a couple of bites from the slice of Early Bird pie Mom offered me. As I chewed, everything that had happened yesterday came back to me full force, and I realized I still hadn't told Mom about the Heartstring recipe. Almost twenty-four hours had passed since I found it.

"Mom," I said around my mouthful of the eggs-and-bacon pie, "there's something I need to tell—"

"Good morning!" Julip's voice drowned out my words as she blew through the door. Following her reluctantly and wearing a grudging frown that told me he'd had a rough twenty-four hours himself, was Chayton.

When he saw me, though, he smiled as if I were the first bright spot he'd had in his morning. I blushed furiously, smiling back.

"Did you oversleep, too?" I whispered teasingly.

"I wish. Family drama." He shrugged, as if it weren't a big deal. But after what I'd overheard between Julip and Mr. Jenkins yesterday, I knew the truth.

He flopped down in the same armchair that I'd just spent the night in, looking as if he just wanted to get this whole thing over with as quickly as possible.

"Julip." The surprise in Mom's voice was obvious. "Is . . . everything all right?"

"Of course it is, silly. Dacey told you, I'm sure, that I wanted to go over the pie contest details with you."

"Oh?" Mom turned to me and I shot her an apologetic look. "Oh. That's right. But . . . I'd got those details pretty much settled—"

"Then this will be quick as a wink," Julip said.

"Mom," I said, easing past Julip, "I've got to go." I glanced at Chayton. "We could walk to school together?"

Chayton opened his mouth, but Julip jumped in with, "That's sweet of you, Dacey, but I need Chayton's help unloading some things from the truck. He'll be at school shortly."

Behind Julip's back, Chayton tugged on his hair and mouthed, *Help me!* I nearly burst out laughing, partly from his theatrics but partly from the relief of knowing that things were still normal between us. Or, as normal as they could be after our almost-kiss. My face flushed, and I realized how much I wanted that almost to become definite.

"Okay," I said to Chayton. "I'll see you later."

I hurried out the door, happier than I'd been in hours. It was only when I was climbing the school steps that I remembered I *still* hadn't told Mom about the Heartstring recipe. Well, I reasoned, the recipe had been waiting for someone to discover it for over forty years. A few more hours wouldn't matter that much.

When I arrived at school, I realized I was very wrong.

The comments started when I reached my locker, where I found a dozen kids waiting.

"Dacey!" Tad offered me a high five. "It's huge news about the pie. Can I swing by the shop after school and grab a slice for my dad? Maybe it will change his mind about my grounding."

"Hey," Caroleen interjected, elbowing Tad, "*I* called the first slice! It's going to get me the solo in the spring glee concert."

Talking over Caroleen was a chorus of other kids, all asking for pie ASAP.

"Guys . . ." I yawned, wondering how I was going to make it through the day on so little sleep. "I'm lost. Which of my mom's pies are you fighting over?"

That curbed them, and they all trained their eyes on me.

"Come on, Dace." Tad laughed. "You were the one who found the recipe." At my confused silence, he added, "Hazel Culpepper's Heartstring Pie?"

The blood rushed from my head to my toes, and I gripped the edge of my locker door, trying to make sense of what he'd just said. "I don't—how do you know about that?"

"*Everybody* knows about it." Caroleen heaved a world-weary sigh, as if this were all completely obvious. "Your bestie's the one who gave us the play-by-play. In today's Buzz?"

I shook my head. That couldn't be right. Zari wouldn't have . . .

Caroleen raised her phone to my face, and Zari's article stared back at me from the screen, the headline announcing: FAMOUS HEARTSTRING PIE REDISCOVERED AT LAST!

I fought the urge to clench my eyes shut, anger broiling inside me.

"So?" Tad persisted. "When can we get our hands on a piece?" He clapped his hands and cried, "Let the healing begin."

I slammed my locker, making them all jump. "That's not how it works," I muttered, pushing past them. Of course, I'd never seen the pie in action, so I couldn't say that for sure. But hadn't GG Hazel been the one who decided who to give the pie to and when? Somehow I didn't think eating it so you could sing in the spotlight or get out of trouble with your parents was what the pie was meant for. Wasn't that why she'd hidden the recipe in the first place, to protect it from situations like this one?

"Come on, Dace, help us out," Tad called after me as I walked down the hall.

I ignored him. My hands trembling, I checked my watch. Five minutes until the bell rang. I turned in the direction of *The Beehive*'s pressroom, my pace quickening as my anger grew.

Zari was exactly where I guessed she'd be, at her press desk about to slip her tablet into her messenger bag. Her burgeoning smile faltered at my frown.

"How could you?" I planted my hands on her desk, staring her down. "You wrote about the Heartstring Pie recipe?"

Zari's eye widened. "Wait . . . you're angry?" She said it with an innocent disbelief that I couldn't fathom.

"I'm furious!" I cried. "You had no right, and you shared it with *everyone*!"

She held up her hands. "Dace, I didn't think it would be a big deal. Everyone was going to find out when you and your mom made the pie anyway. And it's *good* news! Way better than having to report on people selling houses and closing up their restaurants. I thought it would be nice to write about something positive."

"But it was *my* story to tell! My mom's story." I glared at her. "I haven't even had the chance to tell my mom about the recipe yet, and now—" A molten lava of words formed in my mouth. I knew they would sound awful, but the erupting volcano was unstoppable. "Now she'll hear about it from your gossip column! You turned my GG into a cheap tabloid!"

Zari's head flew back as if I'd slapped her, and now her eyes gleamed with as much anger as I felt. "My column's *not* gossip or cheap." She walked around her desk to face me. "I want my writing to be taken seriously—"

"Then don't invade people's privacy!" I threw up my hands. "You never stop to think how it affects people around you! How it feels to be the subject of one of your pieces! You wrote about me and Chayton, and now this! You went too far." I turned away from her. "I don't want to talk to you anymore about anything. I can't ever trust you again. Not when whatever I tell you will end up in your stupid articles."

I stopped, not quite believing that I'd just called Zari's writing "stupid," especially when I knew how much it meant to her. Guilt squeezed my heart, but my anger consumed it.

"Then don't," Zari said. She turned for the door. "Don't tell me anything. I don't want to hear it anyway."

With that, she walked out into the hallway. I stared after her, my eyes pricking with tears. I swiped at them in frustration, then dragged myself to class, dismayed and miserable.

"What happened with you and Zari?" Maria asked as soon as she met me in the cafeteria lunch line.

"Yeah, she texted me a 911 during history class to meet her in the bathroom with tissues." Bree's face crinkled with concern. "She wouldn't tell me what you fought about, only that you weren't going to speak ever again."

"We're not." I spat the words, and Maria lifted her eyebrows. "She messed with GG Hazel. My family. And I can't be friends with someone I can't trust." Maria opened her mouth, and I blurted, "And don't you *dare* tell me to relax, or that it's not a big deal."

"I wasn't going to." Maria voice was resigned, as if she knew nothing she could say to me right now could have any calming effect.

Bree blanched. "But you and Zari can't break up!" She pressed her fingertips against her temples. "I'm a child of divorce. You can't make me choose between the two of you."

Maria rolled her eyes. "Don't freak, Bree. This isn't a divorce. It's just a fight." She scrutinized my expression. "This is about the Heartstring Pie article, I'm guessing?"

"Of course it is!" I snapped. "She had no right to use that story. She didn't even ask me—" My voice cracked with fury, and I didn't trust myself to say anything else.

Bree, ever the peacemaker, chimed in with, "You know Zari's heart is always in the right place even though she can be . . . impulsive about her writing—"

"Look, guys, you don't have to choose between me and Zari. But I don't want to hang out with her anymore." I swallowed. "Ever again."

Maria's eyes widened at my seriousness. "You don't mean that, Dace—"

"I do," I said flatly. I stared at my feet, then put my hand in my shorts pocket. Maybe it was for reassurance or comfort, but I wanted—needed—to feel GG Hazel's recipe there. My body turned ice-cold when my hand found nothing but the empty lining of my pocket. The Heartstring Pie recipe was gone.

I stumbled out of the lunch line, feeling sick to my stomach, nearly dropping my empty tray in my hurry to set it back on the pile with the others.

"Dacey?" Bree said. She and Maria started to follow me, Bree's face pale with worry.

"The recipe," I blurted breathlessly. "I put it in my pocket but it's not there . . ."

"We'll help you look for it," Maria offered, but I shook my head.

"It could've fallen out anywhere between the shop and school. I'll have to retrace my steps," I said, my mind spinning.

"But we still have two more class periods left," Bree started.

"I'll go to the nurse. Say I'm sick." It wasn't even a lie, with the nausea roiling inside me. Then I was jogging toward the cafeteria exit, waving at them over my shoulder. "You have to stay. We can't all go home early. The nurse will never believe us."

I heard Bree call, "Text us later!" as I burst through the door.

But I didn't respond, because I'd slammed into Chayton.

He caught me against him. "We have to quit meeting like this," he said teasingly. He took one glance at my face, and his laughter died.

"What's wrong?" His hands settled on my shoulders in a protective, sweet way that made me want to stay there and tell him everything. Then I thought of Julip Freedell and the hungry persistence she'd been using, bit by bit, to wheedle her way into my mom's trust to gain access to Culpepper recipes. How much more would her persistence grow once she learned I'd found the Heartstring recipe? I imagined her *Prairie Living* crew staking out our house, peering into our windows, jabbing microphones in our faces. My stomach lurched again. No, I decided, it was better to keep this problem from Chayton for now, if only to spare him from his mom's haranguing.

"I—I'm sick," I managed. My face was slick with perspiration. "I'm on my way to the nurse right now."

"Oh, I'm sorry." The worry in his eyes was genuine, and my heart panged at the sight. "Is there anything I can do?"

"I'll be fine." I stepped away. "I should go."

Confusion flashed across his features, and he gave me a questioning look, as if he sensed there was more to what was going on than what I saying. "Okay . . . Feel better?"

I gave him a thumbs-up, then balked internally at the gesture, so out of character for me. I turned before my expression gave anything else away and hurried to Mrs. Hines, the school nurse.

I must have looked awful, because she didn't even bother taking my temperature before calling Mom at the shop.

"Your mom's got some pies about to come out of the oven," Mrs. Hines told me as she hung up. "She said you can wait fifteen minutes for her here, or you can walk, if you feel up to it."

"I can walk," I said, probably a little too hastily. It was in these kinds of moments that I was particularly grateful to live in a place like Bonnet, where no one batted an eye at the idea of a student walking home midday without a ton of paperwork and parental approval forms.

Five minutes later, I carefully retraced my steps from my walk to school that morning, scouring the sidewalk for GG Hazel's recipe. I hoped I'd find it before I had to face Mom.

"Dacey, is that you?" Mom hurried out from the kitchen as soon as she heard the shop door jingle. The shop was more packed with customers than it had been in weeks.

A quick survey of the room—Mrs. Gonzalez's hopeful eyes, Mrs. Beaumont's arthritic hands clasped tightly—and I understood that they'd all heard about the Heartstring Pie. They were waiting for their own slice, just like the kids at school had been.

"Mom—" I started, head bowed.

"Are you all right?" Mom pressed a hand to my forehead, and then, when she had reassured herself that I didn't have a fever, peered into my eyes, confused and excited. "Can you please tell me what's going on? Half of Bonnet has stopped by in the last few hours, asking about Heartstring Pie. I couldn't understand why until Selena showed me Zari's article." She led me behind the display counter and whispered, "Did you really find the recipe?"

"Mom—" For a moment, I couldn't speak. My eyes burned with tears, and I blinked rapidly to keep them from falling. "When the picture frame broke yesterday, I found the recipe hidden inside. I didn't want to tell you in front of Julip's camera crew, and then you were out last night. The recipe was in my pocket, but this morning—" I gulped, hating what I was about to say next. "It must have fallen out when I went to school, or maybe before I left the shop. I don't know. But I don't have it anymore." My lips quivered. "I don't know where it is."

Mom was still as a statue, her eyes downcast, and I waited through the long, torturous seconds as she processed what I'd told her. "Oh," she finally said. Then again, "Oh."

My heart ached. "I'm sorry—"

"Shhhh." She squeezed my hand in hers. "We have to find it, that's all." Her voice was calm and decisive. "We'll retrace your steps and—"

"I already did. The whole way here from school. I looked everywhere." I shook my head. "The only other place to look is the chair. The one I slept in last night."

"Yes!" Mom's face lit up. "Of course! It has to be there!"

With dozen of customers' eyes glued to our every move, Mom and I hurried to the armchair. We lifted the cushions, pressed our hands into the deep recesses of the chair's seams, looking underneath and around it. As we searched, so did everyone else in the shop, checking under tables and napkin dispensers. None of them had to be told what was happening; they all seemed to understand and appeared just as desperate to find the recipe as we were.

When twenty minutes of searching turned up nothing, a mood of mourning settled over the shop. Everyone turned their eyes toward my mother. I understood, more than I ever had before, how much Mom meant to our town. She wasn't only a

Culpepper matriarch, she was a Bonnet one. Even though this was her loss—my family's loss—more than theirs, everyone was waiting, with suspended breath, for her to comfort them, just as she always had.

"Well." She straightened up and cast a smile around the room. "That's that. We've done fine without Heartstring Pie until now, and we'll have to keep doing fine, with . . . or without it." She brushed her hands on her apron, as if she were wiping the last remnants of hope from them. "Now . . . who wants some black-berry ganache?"

No one moved for a long minute, and then slowly, Mrs. Beaumont offered up a soft, "I'll have some. That's always been my favorite anyway."

Within seconds, others were ordering pies, all mustering smiles to let my mom know that they would be all right. *We'll all get through this together*, they seemed to be trying to say. Only they weren't fooling anyone.

Mom turned to me, a trace of sadness in her eyes. "Are you feeling up to helping me, or would you rather go home and rest?"

The way she asked the question, I could tell she knew I wasn't really sick. She was going to let it go, though, which only made my guilt worse.

"I can help," I said, following her into the kitchen.

Once we were alone, I noticed her expression droop with disappointment. "Mom?" My voice came out as a whisper. "I'm so, so sorry."

She pressed a finger to my lips. "It wasn't your fault. Maybe GG Hazel didn't want anyone to find the recipe. Maybe this is fate's way of keeping it a secret forever."

"I don't believe that," I blurted, and Mom looked at me in surprise. "Why would I have found it in the first place if that was what she wanted?" Mom turned away, focusing her attention on adding whipped cream to the top of a chocolate banana cream pie. "You used to say that the recipe was biding its time, waiting for the right person to find it."

"Dacey." Mom sighed. "I remember what I said, but there's nothing to be done about it now." She picked up the pie, then motioned for me to pick up the blackberry ganache pie still sitting on the counter. "Come on. No sense crying over burnt pie."

Normally, I would've rolled my eyes at Mom's corny expression, but I didn't have the heart for it today. *Maybe*, I thought, *my losing the recipe wasn't an accident. Maybe I simply wasn't the right person to find it in the first place.*

Chapter Eleven

The mood in the shop grew more melancholy each time a customer burst in with a request for Heartstring Pie, only to be told that we didn't know when, or if, we'd be able to bake it. I thought about escaping to the stables to ride Ginger but I forced myself to stay at the shop. No matter what Mom said, this *was* my fault, and I was going to help her through it.

I was never happier for closing time to roll around, and it was with a sigh of relief that I finally lifted the OPEN sign from the door, preparing to flip it to CLOSED.

Only I saw one more face waiting behind the glass door.

"What do you want?" My voice was so cold, even to my own ears, that I shivered involuntarily.

"I know you're closing," Zari said, "and I know you hate me right now. But I *need* to come in. It's an emergency."

I hesitated. "I don't want to talk—"

"I know what happened to the recipe," she said. "*Please* let me in."

"Is that Zari?" Mom called from the back of the room, where she was sweeping. "Did she just say something about the Heartstring Pie recipe?"

Reluctantly, I nodded and opened the door, seeing from Mom's anxious expression that I had no choice. Zari rushed inside, pulling her phone from her pocket. She glanced at me sheepishly, then turned to my mom.

"Okay, so after dinner I was scrolling through YouTube, and this video from *Prairie Living* came across my feed." She handed her phone to my mom. "You have to watch it, Miss Edie."

I peered over Mom's and Zari's shoulders as the video began, acutely aware of the tension, heavy as a stone, between Zari and me.

"Hi, y'all, and thanks for watching *Prairie Living*!" Julip beamed from Zari's phone screen, her cheeks rosy and her lips glossed to perfection. "Now I know I don't usually post at this hour, but I have an incredibly exciting announcement to make!" She clapped her hands, obviously thrilled, as the camera panned out to reveal a beautifully wrapped present sitting in Julip's lap. "This coming Saturday—five short days from now—I'll be unveiling the great state of Texas's most legendary pie!"

Her smile broadened as she lifted the lid of the present, reached inside, and pulled out a familiar yellowed piece of paper.

I gasped, my heart stopping in disbelief. "Omigod, that's—"

"Hazel Culpepper's famous Heartstring Pie!" Julip held up the paper, but the writing on it was deftly blurred by the cameras. "This recipe has been hidden for decades, but at last, it's been rediscovered and is ready to share . . ."

Julip went on talking about the legendary healing power of the Heartstring Pie, but her words reached my ears only as the fuzziest of white noise.

"I don't understand," I mumbled through my daze. "How did she even get the recipe in the first place?"

"It doesn't matter." Mom's voice was tired, clipped, and as close to anger as I'd ever heard it. "She has it now, and she's going to squeeze every bit of profit she can out of it."

Zari nodded. "Her plan is to bake the pie during the Bonnet Fair on Saturday, and then she's going to sell the recipe to viewers."

Mom rubbed her forehead as if she had a horrible headache. "She'll probably have all sorts of Heartstring merchandise made up, too. Heartstring Pie pans and T-shirts. Lord knows what else."

"It's horrible," Zari said. "She used you guys to get to the pie recipe."

"Some people just don't know how to respect others' personal lives." I glanced at Zari, frowning. "She wouldn't have even known I'd found the recipe in the first place if *you* hadn't broadcast it to the entire world first."

"Dacey!" Mom scolded. "It's done with now . . ."

185

"Right," I snapped at Zari, "I hope you're happy with the damage you've done."

"Dacey," Mom whispered. "That's enough."

Zari's expression turned from concerned to startled as the full meaning of what I'd just said sank in. "I'm sorry," she whispered. Her mouth caved with hurt. "I . . . should go." There was a tremor in her voice, and my throat squeezed tight. I was still angry, but suddenly, I was ashamed of how vindictive my words had been.

Mom was looking back and forth between us, her eyes full of regret. "Please stop this fighting, girls. It's not what GG Hazel would've wanted."

"That doesn't matter," I said dully. "Not anymore."

Mom sucked in her breath, and I couldn't look at her then, afraid of what I'd see in her face.

"Zari, how about a slice of your favorite Lemon Zinger before you go?" Mom asked, her voice straining toward a false cheeriness.

Zari shook her head. "No, thanks. Not tonight." I thought I glimpsed the shimmer of tears in her eyes. "I . . . wish Julip hadn't done what she did. I wish I didn't have to be the one to tell you about it, either."

Her last words were high and pinched, as if she were trying hard not to cry. The door shut with a click, and less than a second later, Mom's eyes were lasered on me.

"You're too hard on Zari," she said, as if this were just one more problem to add to her already overwhelming plate of troubles for the day. "Everyone makes mistakes, Dace, but your temper—"

"Not now, Mom. Please. I can't talk about it now."

She looked like she wanted to say more, but she nodded.

"I can't believe Julip did this," I said.

"I can't say I'm surprised." Mom shook her head. "Only I wish it hadn't been the Heartstring Pie recipe she got her hands on. Any other recipe, I could've made peace with, but this one." She swallowed. "It's a tough one to take."

My hands balled into fists. "She's a thief! And I still don't know—"

My words hitched in my throat as suddenly, all the pieces of the puzzle fell into place. I thought back to this morning, and I saw the scene replaying before my eyes. I'd fallen asleep with the recipe in my pocket. Julip and Chayton had come into the shop. I'd gotten up from the chair and Chayton had sat down in it. The recipe must have slipped from my pocket when I stood up and then . . . Chayton. He'd sat down in the chair.

I turned to the door. "I have to go. Right now."

"What? Where?" Mom said.

"I'll be home later," was the only way I could think to respond.

I raced for the door, and Mom called after me, "Dad's making dinner tonight. I have to run some pies to Bertie's Waffle House . . ."

"Okay!" I called back.

In seconds, I was rushing to the stables, my fury growing with each stride. I knew exactly how Julip Freedell had ended up with the Heartstring Pie recipe, and I was going to do something about it.

I hurtled into the Jenkins stable, short of breath, my blood howling in my ears. Chayton and Mr. Jenkins looked up, startled, from where they'd been mucking out stalls.

"Hey, Dace!" Chayton held up his hand in a wave, then dropped it just as quickly when he saw my expression.

"Don't you 'Hey' me." I stomped across the hay-strewn ground toward him. "I know what you did."

"Um . . ." Chayton glanced at Mr. Jenkins, who leaned his rake against the wall.

"I have a few things to take care of," Mr. Jenkins said. "I'll be in my office." I didn't wait for him to go before rushing into my next sentence.

"You stole GG Hazel's recipe." The words shot from my mouth like wasps homing in on a target, and Chayton's head snapped back as if they'd hit the mark. "You found it at Pies N' Prattle, didn't you?"

Chayton frowned. "Dace, hang on a sec. I don't even know what you're talking about—"

"You don't know." The sarcasm in my voice was stone-cold. "You don't know that your mother has my family's recipe. That she's planning to bake our Heartstring Pie and sell the recipe on her show?" I closed the distance between us and jabbed an accusatory finger into his chest. "You know because you *gave* her the recipe."

"Dace, listen . . ." He grabbed my hand, but I yanked it from him. His eyes locked on mine. "I didn't take any recipe. I didn't even know you'd found it until I saw Zari's article today at school. And I had no idea about my mom—"

"You're lying." I backed away from him, my throat burning. "You've been lying about everything. You pretended to like me so that you could get close to me." I pressed my hands against my forehead. "God, when we were making that pie, and when you helped me with Ginger . . . Your mom probably put you up to it all."

Chayton's eyes darkened with sadness. "How could you say that?" he asked. "I've been honest with you from the beginning. Why would I have told you that my mom sent me to your shop yesterday if I was trying to help her? You know how frustrated I am with her—how much I hate when she takes advantage of people—"

"I thought I did. I thought I was getting to know you. Until today." I glared at him. "You used me."

Chayton stared at the ground for a long second, and then kicked at his pile of straw, sending it flying. "You've already decided not to believe me."

"Why should I believe you? You don't have any idea what loyalty and friendship are." I spat the words. "You never have."

Chayton sighed. "I thought we were past all of this, Dace. We were heading in a good direction. Maybe even great. But . . . there's nothing I can say, is there?" The hurt shone in his eyes. "There's this pattern you have. Someone makes a mistake, and you get angry. Only you don't let go of your anger. You say hurtful things, and you leave the rest of us to wait it out, thinking we'll eventually forget about it."

"So you admit you made a mistake," I persisted. "You took the recipe."

"That's the only part of what I said that you heard, wasn't it?" He picked up his rake. "You made up your mind about me a long time ago," he said softly. "I should've known you couldn't change it."

"Why would I change it? You're just another of your mom's puppets, doing whatever she wants, no matter what the price."

An odd look crossed his face then, as if a door was closing over it, shutting me out. Then, without another word, he turned from me, resuming his work.

I backed toward the doors of the stable, passing Ginger's stall. I glanced in her direction. She was watching me with her huge, velvet eyes, but the confusion I saw in them cut me to the quick.

What had I just said? Stark regret blistered my insides and tears pricked my eyes. What had I just done? I stumbled out of the stables, hoping I'd at least make it home before the waterworks began.

I didn't hear my cell phone the first few times, but at last, its ringing broke through my daze.

"Dacey?" Dad's voice was strained. "Where are you?"

"Dad?" My heart, already pounding, broke into a gallop. "What's wrong?"

"I just got a call from Mr. Victor." His voice broke. "Your mom's been in a car accident. She's all right but banged up pretty good. He's taking her to Bonnet Hospital. I'm meeting them there—"

"Wait for me." My tears were falling now. "I'm coming home."

I didn't wait for Dad's response. I didn't wait another second. I ran.

I stared at my phone screen, the Candy Crush game flashing its fluorescent colors. I'd thought I'd be able to do something mindless while I waited for Dad to come back to the tiny waiting room, but I couldn't even concentrate enough to play the stupid game. Of course, that might've had something to do with the fact that every few seconds, my phone buzzed with another text from someone asking after Mom. The first three had been from Zari, Bree, and Maria, but as the Bonnet phone tree worked its magic, more and more messages streamed in from Mrs. Gonzalez, Mrs. Beaumont, Mr. Jenkins . . . Even Chayton had texted, but his was the simplest, only four words long: HOPE EVERYTHING IS OK.

He probably didn't expect, or even want, a response, and I didn't want to give him one. He'd get news through the Bonnet grapevine soon enough anyway.

I put down my phone, giving up on the game, and stood up to pace. But the room was so small all I could really do was turn in a small circle. The Bonnet Hospital was an old nineteenth century farmhouse that Doctor Higgins and his team of nurses and physician's assistants had converted into a medical facility. There was a bigger, proper hospital an hour's drive away for more complicated surgeries and treatments, but this one got the job done when it came to delivering babies, removing tonsils, and setting broken bones.

I could hear Dad's and Doctor Higgins's voices through the paper-thin walls, and I took it as a good sign when I heard a low rumble of laughter from Doctor Higgins. Still, my stomach spun uneasily.

My thoughts over the last hour had run on a repeating loop: Mom, Heartstring Pie, Chayton, Zari . . . Mom, Heartstring Pie, Chayton, Zari. My mind couldn't decide what to focus on—worry, guilt, or anger—so it was dividing itself equally between the three. The one thing it had decided on, though, was that somehow, everything that had happened in the last twenty-four hours was my fault.

That verdict was so consuming that I didn't see Dad until he was beside me, making me jump.

"How's Mom?" I asked instantly.

"She'll be fine. She's got a mild concussion and a broken collarbone. Bed and brain rest until the end of the week, and she'll be right as rain." He smiled. "She's more worried about that pig than she is about herself. Of course, your mom's so bighearted, she would've run herself off the road to save a cockroach, let alone a pig." He gave a tired laugh as he sank into one of the waiting room chairs. "Mr. Victor must have apologized to me a hundred times before he went home."

"Well, Tootsie was the one that ran right in front of Mom's car! Again! For the hundredth time!"

Dad nodded. "And she'll probably do it again. That pig is one master escape artist. But your mom admitted she was distracted. Didn't see Tootsie until it was almost too late . . ."

My stomach lurched. "Was she thinking about the Heartstring Pie recipe?" I asked softly, sitting down beside him.

Dad shrugged. "She didn't say."

"I know she was. She's so disappointed that the recipe's gone." I sucked in a breath as tears filled my eyes. "And I'm the one who lost it—"

"Oh, Honeybee." Dad put his arm around me, kissing my forehead. "These things just happen. Recipes get lost, bones get broken . . ." He chuckled. "Pigs go rogue. There's no sense in wishing life is something different than it is."

"But I do."

"I'll let you in on a secret," Dad said. "We grown-ups say these supposedly wise things, but in the end, there are plenty of times we wish things could be different, too." He brushed gently at my tears with his hand.

"But the recipe could've helped the shop," I hiccupped.

"Maybe. Maybe not." He tucked my head under his chin and we sat like that for several minutes before he added, "The shop's brought a lot of people joy and maybe even a measure of healing. Soul soothing, as your mom likes to say. But there are times I've wished your mom wasn't so attached to it, when I wished she could be free of the responsibility she feels for it."

"Me too," I confessed in a whisper. "Maybe she would be, if I could do more at the shop. I just want to help somehow."

"You're here. You love her. That's helping enough."

I shook my head. "But if I could actually bake . . ."

Dad sighed. "Dace, you've got to quit focusing on your *cant's*. Your mom can bake, but she can't ride a horse for the life of her, so you've got her there."

I smiled, remembering the last time Mom tried to ride Ginger and ended up falling off, right into the Brazos. "True."

"And your legendary GG Hazel? She was a terrible nurse."

I stared at him. "No way."

Dad nodded vehemently. "Couldn't stand the sight of blood, but she still wanted to do her part for the war effort. She didn't say a word to the Red Cross about her squeamishness, either. She was determined to get past it. The head nurses, though, they figured it out soon enough."

"But what about the story of how she helped the wounded soldiers at Normandy Beach?"

"Oh, she was at Normandy," Dad said, "but not dressing wounds. She handed out food and blankets, and they put her to work cooking, too."

"What about her baking?" I asked.

"That came after she got back to the States." Dad grinned. "As it turned out, she had a knack for baking pies, and the rest is history."

I let this news sink in. "Why didn't Mom ever tell me?"

"I'm not sure. Maybe she got so caught up in the legend of Hazel Culpepper that she forgot who Hazel was as a person. Or maybe she was worried that if you knew you'd give up trying to bake."

"GG Hazel's failure at nursing would have given me permission to fail at baking?" Even as I said it out loud, I wondered if it might've done that very thing. If it might've given me an excuse to quit. But after sitting with GG Hazel's story for a minute, I realized that it wasn't having that effect on me at all.

"Well, don't be mad at Mom for not telling you before, okay?" Dad said. "She's your biggest fan, and whatever her reasons, she was only trying to help."

"I'm not mad. I feel . . . better." I said it with some surprise. Knowing that GG Hazel wasn't perfect, that there was something she hadn't excelled at, was strangely soothing.

"Good." Dad hugged me, then stood up. "Mom's sleeping now, and Doctor Higgins wants to keep her overnight to monitor her concussion. Why don't I take you home? Mom asked me to bring her favorite fuzzy pajamas, so I'll pack a few things and bring them back after I get you settled for the night."

I nodded, and we moved toward the door. Suddenly, I was struck with an idea.

"Dad, can you drop me at Pies N' Prattle on your way home? There's something I need to do."

"Sure," he answered. "But you go straight home afterward. I've arranged for Mrs. Beaumont to stay overnight with you while I'm with Mom. I don't want her worrying—"

"It'll only take a couple hours, and I'll check in with Mrs. Beaumont while I'm there. Oh . . . and Dad? Can we swing by Bonnet Grocery on the way? I need some Heath bars."

Dad stared at me, then laughed. "What on earth for?"

"Can't tell you. Not yet."

"I should've known better than to ask." He grinned, then hugged me. "Clearly you're a girl on a mission. And you've never reminded me more of your mom."

I smiled. "Thanks."

We stepped into the balmy night air, and a few lightning bugs flickered their welcome as we walked to the car. My heart buoyed a bit at the sight of them. There were still so many unknowns, so many doubts. The one thing I felt certain about, though, was Mom. She took care of most of the town, of Dad, of me. Maybe there was something I could do to take care of her, now that she needed it. I just had to find the courage to give it a try.

Chapter Twelve

There was a warmth to the air inside Pies N' Prattle when I stepped through the door, and I felt a gentle easing of my nerves. The shop didn't fill me with trepidation like it usually did, or with reminders of the abilities I lacked. Instead, it felt welcoming, as if it knew what I'd come here to do.

Even though Mom wasn't here, there were signs of her everywhere. Her apron hanging on the hook, the nearly empty glass of iced tea she'd left on the counter. It was comforting, and for the first time, so was seeing the photo of GG Hazel on the wall.

I smiled, feeling a kinship with my great-grandmother that I'd never felt before. I knew one of her failings now, and she seemed human, more real. With her determined eyes and the slightly crooked bend in her smile, she looked—I finally noticed with amazement—a little like me. How *had* I never seen the resemblance before?

My hand was steady as I pressed my palm against the faded photograph.

"Let me help one heart tonight," I whispered, then added my mom's words, feeling their conviction coursing through me. "Then more hearts tomorrow, GG. I promise."

I stared into her eyes and thought I saw approval in them, as if we'd reached an understanding. I didn't wait for second guesses or doubts, but went straight into the kitchen. I busied myself turning on the oven and gathering ingredients. Each time thoughts of Julip Freedell's video, or my fights with Chayton or Zari slunk into my head, I shoved them away. Tonight was about Mom, GG Hazel, and me—the three of us.

First, I mixed the chocolate chip cookie dough, adding in the hefty helping of crushed Heath bars, just like GG Hazel's recipe called for. I'd looked at the recipe so many times, I remembered much of it, but not the exact measurements. And the rest? Well, if GG had invented her own unique version of Chess pie in the first place, why couldn't I invent mine? It wouldn't be exactly like GG Hazel's, but maybe, I wondered, after all the feuding over her recipe, that was what she'd wanted? For someone to come along who could put enough heart into the pie to make it her own?

I smiled to myself as I stirred the Heath bar in, wondering how Hazel had thought of that ingredient in the first place. I hadn't even known they'd had Heath bars in the 1940s, and I made a mental note to ask Mom about it later.

I slid the cookies into the oven, and as I waited for them to bake, I mixed the pie filling. Some of the ingredients— buttermilk, eggs, sugar, vanilla—were the same ones Mom used in her Chess pie. As I mixed, a small voice whispered in my head that it wasn't quite right. Not for the Dacey Culpepper Biel version. Then it came—inspiration, sweet and bright as my great-grandmother's hug might've been. Feeling excited, I poured in two scoops of dark chocolate morsels, plus another hefty helping of crushed Heath. It was different than any recipe

I'd ever seen Mom make, but that seemed to make it easier for *me* to bake it. This time, I wasn't comparing my skill to anyone else's. This time, it was just me, alone in Pies N' Prattle. Only I didn't feel alone. I felt myself surrounded by the memories of the women who'd been here before me. They weren't judging but guiding, like footprints I was stepping in to get where I wanted to be.

As I worked, the kitchen filled with the buttery, chocolatey scent of fresh-baked cookies, and when I pulled them from the oven, they were golden-brown perfection. Yes! So far, so good. I cautiously bit into one and smiled. They tasted even better than they looked.

Once they'd cooled enough, I crumbled the cookies into a bowl and then spooned in softened butter until the mixture solidified enough that I could press it into the bottom of the pie pan for the crust. Then, with steady hands, I carefully poured the pie filling into the pan, and slid the pie into the oven. For some long seconds, I held my breath, waiting—and dreading, too. The stories of Culpepper curses were hornets in my head, peskily buzzing. I'd gone rogue, and it had felt right, but it might (quite literally) blow up in my face. Food poisoning, a fire, a—gulp—mouse? All had happened to Culpeppers before me . . . but—

"No!" I said out loud, startling myself. "Be quiet!" It wasn't directed at GG Hazel, but to the aunts, cousins, strangers who'd tried to make her pie for all the wrong reasons, or tried for the right reasons but maybe at the wrong time. "This is *my* pie, and you'll let it be!"

The words echoed in the kitchen for a moment, and then all was quiet—the shop and the whispers in my head. And that was when I laughed at the ridiculousness of what I'd just done, but also at the bravery of it. Maybe—just this once—my temper would prove a help to me.

With the inexplicable but solid sense that I'd somehow set something to rights, I went into the main room and curled up in an armchair to wait for the pie to finish baking. I pulled out my phone from my pocket to check in with Mrs. Beaumont, but I saw a barrage of texts. There were several from Bree and Maria and a dozen texts and two voice mails from Zari, begging me for info on my mom. My heart ached when I heard the concern in Zari's voice, and I began to dial her cell, then stopped.

I knew that Zari's concern for Mom was genuine, just like I knew that Zari's "tabloid" reporting was really her outlet for the frustration of living in a town she felt she was outgrowing. But none of that changed the fact that she'd gone too far. I wasn't sure I could trust her anymore, but if I couldn't, how could the two of us stay best friends?

Finally I opted to text both Bree and Maria one simple message: MOM WILL BE FINE. I'M FINE, TOO. TALK MORE 2MRW. I knew the lack of details would disappoint them, but it was all I was up to right now. They'd tell Zari, I was sure. I wasn't ready to talk to her yet. I wasn't sure when I would be. *If* I would be. The thought saddened me. To distract myself from it, I called Mrs. Beaumont, telling her I'd be home in about an hour, and then my phone dinged one more time.

My heart jumped when I saw it was a text from Chayton:

HEARD YOUR MOM IS ALL RIGHT. WANTED TO CALL, BUT I KNOW YOU DON'T WANT ME TO. YOU WANT ME TO LEAVE YOU

ALONE, SO I WILL. FROM NOW ON. I JUST WANTED TO TELL
YOU THAT I'M SORRY. ABOUT YOUR MOM. ABOUT EVERYTHING.

I sat back in the armchair, staring at the text. My eyes welled
up again, but whether the tears were from anger or sadness, I
wasn't sure. Chayton was apologizing for everything, which had
to mean he was admitting he'd taken the recipe. Only, now that
I was calmer and my initial fury had left me, the idea didn't sit
right with me.

He'd worked so hard to earn my trust over the last few weeks.
More than that, he'd told me he *liked* me. We'd almost kissed.
Had it all been a performance? A ruse?

The timer beeped in the kitchen, pulling me from my
thoughts. I glanced at Chayton's text one last time, then deleted
it. Swallowing down my mixed feelings, I made my way to the
kitchen, wondering if I'd be met with a rotten-socks stench that
meant the "curse" had struck again.

But when I opened the oven door, I was met with an other-
worldly aroma—toffee, chocolate, and butter bliss. There it
was—baked to a scrumptious golden color with bits of melted

toffee and chocolate freckling the top. I smiled. I'd done it. The first pie I'd ever successfully baked, and one nobody had succeeded in baking in nearly half a century. It was GG Hazel's famous Heartstring Pie.

I woke from a deep, dreamless sleep to the sound of Dad's truck rumbling into our driveway. I sat up and took in the late morning sunlight slanting through my bedroom window, then glanced at my clock. It was eleven a.m.!

I heard familiar voices in the kitchen—Mrs. Beaumont's . . . and Mom's! My heart scampered. Mom was home from the hospital. A minute later, I saw Mrs. Beaumont walking down our front walk and onto Main Street.

I swung my legs over the side of the bed. For a minute I wondered if my midnight baking spree at Pies N' Prattle had only been a dream. But no . . . there was the Heartstring Pie on my windowsill, looking just as picture-perfect in daylight as it had when I'd pulled it from the oven.

I dressed, scooped up the pie, and went in search of Mom. I was relieved to find her nestled in bed. Her left arm, in its cast, was propped up on pillows. Even though she was pale, she was looking mostly perky. Dad was busy setting up a small folding bed tray for her.

"Hey, Honeybee," Dad said to me. "I'm gonna fix your mom some breakfast, and then I'll take you to school. I already called and told them you'd be late." He added, with a wink in Mom's direction, "Try to keep her resting, will ya?"

Sure enough, the second Dad was gone, Mom whispered, "I'm already plotting my escape."

I laughed. "I figured as much. I'm so glad you're okay," I added, feeling a lump in my throat as I moved toward her.

"Course I am. Tootsie hasn't seen the end of me yet." She shifted against her pillows, then winced. "She did manage to give me a whopper of a headache, though."

"It still hurts?"

"Doctor Higgins says it will for a few days. The more rest I get, the faster I'll heal."

I sucked in a breath, seeing the opportunity I'd been waiting for. "Well, I made you something that I hope might help." I pulled the pie from behind my back and set it on the bed tray.

Mom stared down at it, her expression pleased and surprised. "Dacey! You baked this beautiful pie?"

"I know! Crazy, right? Nothing burned or crumbled. Or imploded. Last night, I wanted to do something for you. And I realized I remembered some of the recipe, and I improvised a little—"

"Wait." Mom's eyes widened. "Are you saying that this . . . this is—"

"Heartstring Pie."

Mom gasped. "And nothing happened to you? To it?" Worry clouded her eyes.

I laughed. "Nothing yet."

"B-but that's never happened before—"

"Shhhh!" I interrupted, "Don't jinx it!"

Mom nodded, staring at the pie, then giggling in a way that made her sound much younger than she was. "Dacey, I can't believe it." She covered her mouth with her hand, tearing up. "You actually baked GG Hazel's pie."

My cheeks flushed. "I haven't tasted it yet. But, I don't know, I think it's going to be okay. I really do. I feel it . . ."

"Jim?" Mom called out to my dad. "We need some forks."

Not a minute later, Dad reappeared holding the forks, his eyebrows raised in question. When he noticed the pie, his jaw dropped. "That's not—"

"It is. And we're going to taste it." Mom held out her hand for the forks. "Alone." She gave Dad a pointed but affectionate look that clearly said, *Girl time.*

"Your wish is my command, your majesty." Dad grinned, bowing as he placed the forks in her hand, and then backed out of the room, still bowing.

I felt a wave of love toward them both: toward Mom, for understanding that if something was wrong with this pie, I'd want it to stay between the two of us. And toward Dad, for taking her cue, no questions asked.

Mom and I looked at each other, then at the pie. "On the count of three?" I suggested.

"One. Two," Mom counted.

"Three!" we said together, then dipped our forks into the pie. I closed my eyes and opened my mouth, not daring to look at how the pie held together on my fork. The bite was smooth and chewy all at once, with vanilla custard undertones and chocolate and toffee accents. The crust gave it just the right amount of cookie crunch.

It was . . . good. Really, really good.

"*Yum,*" I breathed, diving in for a second taste.

"Yum is right." Mom took a hefty second scoop of pie, slid it into her mouth, and then leaned back against her pillows, beaming. "Dace. It's incredible."

I started to argue, but found that I couldn't. Besides, my mouth was too full of pie. I started giggling, half in shock. "I guess it is," I managed to reply.

"You did it." Mom's face glowed with pride. "You broke the curse."

I swallowed down the piece of pie. "If there ever *was* a curse."

"Hush, Hazel might be listening," Mom said teasingly. "How *did* you do it?"

I tried to explain. "All the other times I've baked, I tiptoed through the recipe like it was a minefield or something. This time, I got caught up in the moment, and . . ." I shrugged. "I forgot to tiptoe." I took another bite of pie, letting it melt in my mouth. "Mmmm. It's got the gooeyness of cookies straight out of the oven."

"Maybe that's why the boys returning home from the war loved it so much," Mom said as she chewed.

"Because it made them remember being kids?" I suggested.

"Or it made them remember simple pleasures."

We were digging into the pie properly now, making a big gap in the middle. "Do you think this is how they ate it? Straight out of the pie pan?" I asked.

"I don't know, but with a pie that tastes this good, it would've been hard to wait for a proper slice." We laughed, and then Mom set down her fork and slid her hand over mine, looking serious. "Dace, I owe you an apology."

"Why?"

"I think maybe, without meaning to, I've been putting pressure on you." I opened my mouth, but Mom hushed me. "No. Let me say this. Please." She held my gaze. "Even before you were born, I had this idea of what I wanted for you. I had this picture of you and me baking, side by side. Keeping GG Hazel's dreams alive together." She cocked her head. "I'm not sure why parents do that to their kids, but we do. We have expectations, dreams we want them to fulfill, long before they even have a say in the matter." Her eyes welled. "And the bakery meant so much to me, I was so sure you'd love it, too." She leaned toward me, squeezing my hand. "But I promise you that if you don't, it's okay. I love you, and I could never force you to do something you didn't find joy in—"

"Mom," I interrupted quietly. "I do love the bakery. So, so much." I heaved a breath. "That's why it killed me that I couldn't bake. This whole time, I felt like I was letting you down.

Disappointing you, and Grandma, and GG Hazel. Like I was the first Culpepper failure."

"No—" Mom looked horrified by the thought.

"But," I continued, "it wasn't *you* who pressured me. I did it to myself. And when I failed . . ." I sighed. "Well. My temper never helped much." I shrugged. "I see that now, because last night, when I was alone in the bakery, I forgot about being nervous, and all the times I'd messed up recipes. For the first time, I felt like I was a part of the Culpepper tradition instead of standing outside of it. Everything just . . . clicked."

I let out a breath, and Mom pulled me into a hug with her good arm. "Oh, Dacey, I'm so sorry you felt that way. And I'm so glad you told me." She kissed my cheek.

"There's something else, Mom." I smiled. "I think I figured out what GG's words meant. When she said, 'The secret to the sweetest of pies is hidden in the heart of Bonnet'?" Mom nodded expectantly. "She meant love. To her, love was the sweetest of pies. It was what she put into her Heartstring Pie that made people feel better."

"I know you're right." Mom's eyes got even tearier, and she hugged me again. "It's the sweetest of pies for me, too, Dace. For all of us. I'm proud of you, and . . ." She pointed at the pie. ". . . I cannot believe how delicious your pie is."

"GG Hazel's pie," I corrected, but Mom shook her head.

"It's yours now, too, Dace. You found the recipe and you were the first one to bake it after all these years." She brushed away her tears, smiling, and sat back. "You know what I think? I think GG Hazel meant for you to find it. I really do."

I felt a little shiver of joy, but then I giggled. "I don't know, Mom. You also believe her spirit lives in a 1940s newspaper clipping."

"I do *not*," Mom protested, then added quietly, "most of the time."

We laughed, and then I sobered as a new thought struck me. "Mom, the Bonnet Fair's this Saturday. The pies for the pie-eating contest—"

"I know." Mom plucked a piece of Heartstring Pie crust from the pan and popped it into her mouth, closing her eyes as she relished its flavor. "I won't be able to bake the pies. If I did, my concussion would last longer. Brain rest means no books, no TV . . ." She sighed. "No baking."

"Everyone will understand."

Mom scoffed. "I know one person who won't."

"Julip." Just saying her name made anger rise in my throat. "But she's already got her golden ticket. The Heartstring Pie recipe." My hands tightened to fists at the thought.

"Dacey." Mom's voice held a note of warning. "I don't like what she did, either. But on a scale of one to ten, split ends to bubonic plague, this is—"

"A ten," I finished.

"Not even a five," Mom corrected. "There are so many worse things that could happen." She gave me a look. "There's nothing like having a near miss with a five-hundred-pound pig to keep things in perspective. I'm okay. I have you and your dad. And we have the shop."

"But, Mom, business is still slowing, and if more people move out of town, then—"

"Then we'll see. We'll do our best and see what happens. I don't want to lose the shop, but I—we—will get through it. And . . ." She gestured to the pie. ". . . we have this amazing pie. It's already making me feel better. It truly is." She took another enormous bite. "Ith reabby ish sho good," she mumbled around her mouthful.

We laughed, and I hugged her. "Love you."

"You too."

"Whoa," Dad's voice came from the doorway. We glanced up to see him holding a plate of eggs and bacon while he eyed the remains of the pie. "A half-finished pie in under five minutes? That's a good sign."

Mom's eyes shone with a pride that made me blush. "Just look at the Heartstring Pie our daughter made."

"Oh, I'll do more than look." Dad set the plate down on the dresser, then swooped over and snatched the fork from my hand, nudging me off the bed.

"Hey!" I protested as he dug into the pie. "Did you forget you're supposed to take me to school?"

"Nu-uh." He shook his head. "Mr. Jenkins stopped by and offered to take you. He's waiting for you in the kitchen."

Mr. Jenkins? I was filled with an instant dread at the idea of seeing him after all the things I'd said to Chayton in the stable yesterday. But I made my expression a mask of composure, not wanting to give Mom anything to worry about except her recovery.

Dad took a bite of the pie and closed his eyes. "Bliss! Euphoria!" I started to laugh, but then Dad opened one eye. "Be gone with you. I'm *very* busy taking care of your mother."

"More like busy eating pie." Mom blew me a kiss. "See you after school."

I walked to the kitchen, listening to my parents' voices hitting happy notes as they talked. I didn't know if it was the simple fact that I'd baked it, or if it really did have some sort of inexplicable knack for healing, but that pie had a way of cheering people up. Even as I reached the kitchen and saw Mr. Jenkins standing there, clutching his Stetson in his hands, even as my heart jittered at his steady, almost stern gaze—a strange peace was settling over me, an assurance that like Mom said, everything would be all right in the end.

"Dacey." Mr. Jenkins gave a single nod. "I brought some flowers for your mom, and Mazie made her pulled pork casserole for y'all. Your dad put it in the fridge for later."

"Thank you, Mr. Jenkins," I said, having trouble meeting his eyes. I shifted my feet, wanting nothing more than to be out from under his scrutiny. "I'll just grab my school stuff and—"

"Hold tight there." He patted the counter with his palm. "I've got something I need to get off my chest."

I swallowed. *Here it comes*, I thought. *The lecture.* "Mr. Jenkins," I blurted. "If you don't want me to board Ginger at your stables anymore, I'll understand. But I won't take back the things I said to Chayton. I can't when they were every ounce the truth—"

"They weren't, though," he said. "That's what I came to tell you." He rubbed his stubbled chin. "Chayton didn't take Hazel's recipe. Julip did."

I stared at him in shock. "Wh-what?"

He nodded. "I heard her on the phone Sunday evening. She

was talking to the *Prairie Living* producer. Not an upstanding man, but that's neither here nor there. Point is she was telling him about her plan to get the show's ratings back on top. She said she had the Heartstring Pie recipe in hand. That your mom had given it to her, along with permission to share it on the show."

"But Mom didn't give it to her! The recipe fell out of my pocket somehow, and then—"

"I know." Mr. Jenkins held up his hand. "Julip found it and got greedy." He sighed, and his weathered face suddenly looked much older. "I'm sorry for all of it," he said quietly. "The whole darned mess."

"It's not your fault." I felt a pang of sympathy for him. I'd always liked Mr. Jenkins, and it was hard to see him—usually so upright and sturdy—looking ashamed. "Besides, there's nothing we can do about it now, and Mom's okay with that. *We're* okay with that. Really." What I needed to say next wasn't easy, and the embarrassment of having to admit how wrong I'd been was like nettles under my skin. That was one thing I for sure had inherited from the Culpepper matriarchs—a stubborn resistance to confessing mistakes. "I shouldn't have accused Chayton the way I did. It wasn't fair."

Mr. Jenkins's piercing eyes told me what he thought about the way I'd treated Chayton. "That's between you and my grandson to work out. I know better than to step in a snake's nest." He put his hat on, the signal that it was time to go. "Best get you to school now."

I gathered my stuff as a dervish of emotions whirled inside me. *Chayton*. His name was like a sad song I couldn't quit humming.

The ride to school was quiet, except for the Johnny Cash music Mr. Jenkins had playing. It was only when I was already halfway out the passenger door that Mr. Jenkins called after me.

"My daughter and I don't see eye to eye on many things." His voice was sad. "But Chayton is not his mother. That boy's been sweet on you since you wore pigtails. All he ever wanted was a chance. But don't let on I told you so."

Without another word, he reached across the truck's cab, swung my door shut, and drove away, leaving me behind with my crumbling heart.

Chapter Thirteen

I stood on the sidewalk, stunned and gutted by Mr. Jenkins's words. The entire world seemed different, as if a curtain had lifted on my true feelings. But . . . was it too late to do anything about it? My stomach twisted. It couldn't be.

I hurried through the school doors. Lunch period was over, and the hallways swarmed with kids heading to their lockers. I scanned the faces for Chayton's, but I didn't see him anywhere.

I remembered he had biology after lunch and turned toward the science department—but slammed straight into Zari.

The disappointment at what she'd done stung fresh. I took a step back, but she grabbed my hands in hers.

"Dace, wait." Her lips trembled. "Please. Can we talk for a second?"

I shrugged but didn't turn away. One thing the last twenty-four hours had taught me was that I'd made plenty of mistakes and I was hoping to be forgiven for them. But how could I hope for that myself and refuse it to Zari? I had to hear what she had to say.

"I'm sorry," she said softly. "I should've asked you before I wrote the article about Hazel's recipe. I got so carried away with the idea that I finally had a legit news story to report . . . I forgot that it was your story to tell."

"It was more than mine. It belonged to my mom, too. And now . . . well, she doesn't even get to have a moment with it to herself. Not with what Julip's planning to do."

"I know." Zari bit her lip. "It's horrible. And I don't want to be like that—snatching what's important to people and turning it into gossip."

"You mean you don't want to be a reporter anymore?" I asked doubtfully.

"Oh no!" Zari said. "I want to be a reporter, but I want to do right by the people I report about. I'll ask permission to tell their stories and—" She shot me a penitent look. "Respect their privacy whenever I can."

I nodded.

"Unless it involves another Tootsie escape," she added hurriedly. "That's a matter of public safety."

"I'll give you that." We both laughed, and some of the tension between us evaporated. Still, I felt a lingering doubt. "You broke my trust." My voice was quiet. "It might take some time to earn it back."

"I know, and I want to make it right," Zari insisted. "I'll understand if you can't talk to me about everything. But when you're ready, I promise not to share anything you don't want me to. Not ever again."

I took a deep breath. "Okay. When I'm ready."

She gave me a steady look, then added, "I've never seen you that mad before. At least not at me."

I felt a sharp pang in my chest. "I know." My cheeks flamed. "I totally lost it, and . . . I know how awful I sounded. I said things I didn't mean. I'm sorry, and I'm going to try not to let it happen again."

She nodded. "Cause the Hulk is scary."

We both laughed again, and then we were hugging and smiling, the way we'd done since we were little. There was a cautiousness to it, as if we might need to handle each other with extra care for a while. But I guess that was how it worked in rough patches of friendship. We'd find normal again, even if it took some time.

"So your mom is okay, right?" Zari asked. "I heard through the grapevine that she was, but I want to hear it from a primary source."

"She's fine." As Zari walked with me to the office for my late pass, I filled her in on Mom's status and on my baking victory with the Heartstring Pie. "I just wish there was a way to stop Julip from sharing the recipe at the fair. It'll be all over social media and there's nothing we can do about it."

After I got my pass, we left the office and turned toward our lockers. Then Zari froze midstep. "What if there *is* something we can do? What if we beat Julip at her own game?" Her eyes lit up with excitement.

"What do you mean?" I asked.

"I mean that we share the recipe on social media before she does."

My brow furrowed. "But I don't want to share the recipe."

"We won't share the whole thing." She grinned. "Just enough to get people craving more."

"Okay," I said slowly. "I'm listening."

Zari explained her idea as we walked to class, and the more I heard, the more I liked it. In fact, I was 100 percent on board with the plan until Zari said that we'd need Chayton's help. "It will have way more impact if Julip Freedell's son is involved. In a way, it will seem like it's sanctioned by *Prairie Living*."

My face fell. "I'm not sure Chayton will want to help."

Zari's brow furrowed. "Why not?"

"Because I might've called him a thief? And a liar?" I squeaked out.

"Da—cey." Zari slapped her hand to her forehead. "Why?"

"Because I wasn't thinking straight, and I jumped to the wrong conclusions, and—"

"You lost your temper," Zari said matter-of-factly.

"I lost my temper." I sighed. "But I need to talk to him. Explain everything . . ." The bell rang then, cutting me off.

"We've got to go," Zari said. "Class is starting."

I nodded reluctantly. "If you see him before I do, tell him—"

Zari shook her head, walking away from me. "Oh no. Nu-uh. I'm not telling him anything. No more spilling secrets, remember? This is all you. But let me know when the groveling's over. If he decides not to despise you for all eternity, we have planning to do." She grinned and offered me a thumbs-up, then dipped into her English classroom.

If he decides not despise you. That was a big "if." The bigger question, though, was: What if he already did?

I waited at Chayton's locker between fifth and sixth periods, hoping I might catch him there. My breath hitched when I spotted him walking toward me with JC and Tad, and—oh no—Caroleen.

Caroleen had her arm through his, whispering something in his ear, in full flirt mode. Chayton's expression was distracted, though, and he seemed to be only half listening to her. Suddenly his eyes caught mine and he stopped, quickly turning away, deciding that it was better to avoid his locker entirely than speak to me.

I called after him, but it was Tad who answered, giving me an apologetic shrug and saying, "Leave it alone, Dace. You've done enough already."

If I'd been kicked in the stomach, it wouldn't have knocked the wind out of me more than Tad's words did. A chilling fear slunk over me, and for the first time I thought about the very real possibility that, no matter what I did or said, Chayton might never want anything to do with me again. How many times had I misjudged him? He'd already offered me more chances than I deserved.

Then I remembered Mr. Jenkins. He had always been a man of few words. If it were utterly hopeless, if I had no chance with Chayton, why would he have bothered saying what he'd said to me earlier?

After school, I walked straight to the Jenkins ranch. When I reached the stables, Flash's stall was empty, and Chayton's saddle was missing from the tack room. My heart fluttered. I knew where to find him.

I saddled Ginger and rode her out to the trail along the Brazos. As I urged Ginger from a canter to a gallop and we picked up speed, I tried to bolster my nerves, rehearsing what I wanted to say in whispers that the wind swept away. Eventually, I eased Ginger into a walk as we wove between the live oaks and down the embankment to the water's edge.

I caught sight of Chayton sitting in the cradle of the heart-shaped oak. Flash was tied to a branch nearby while Chayton skipped stones in the river. Blood rushed to my cheeks as I watched the way his forearms flexed with each toss, the way his black curls fell across his forehead. How had there ever been a time when I *hadn't* thought he was cute? His cuteness, though, wasn't even a close match to his kindness and his humor. It seemed ridiculous to me now that I could ever have found him annoying.

I might've stayed there, admiring him from a distance, but Flash noticed us, perking his ears, snorting and sidestepping to announce our arrival.

Chayton looked up and a myriad of emotions swept his face—surprise, then happiness, followed by hostility. He turned away, focusing his attention on the river again.

"Why are you here?" he muttered.

"Can I talk to you?" I slid from my saddle and tethered Ginger to a spot close, but not too close, to Flash. I moved to where Chayton was sitting and picked up a few stones myself. I tossed one and watched it skim the water and take four little leaps before sinking. Chayton followed suit, but his rock made six skips.

"Impressive," I said. "But I bet you can't make it all the way across."

I held my breath, hoping he might play along. Instead, he dropped his handful of rocks.

"Don't do that," he said quietly. "Don't pretend like everything's all right between us." He dug the toe of his boot into the dirt. "I'm tired of it, Dace. Me always trying, always laughing and joking, and you always—"

"Picking fights?" I offered. "Accusing you of things you didn't do? Losing my temper?"

He looked momentarily surprised, but then his frown returned. "All of the above," he mumbled resignedly.

"That's fair." I nodded. "And you're right to be sick of it. I'm sick of me right now, too."

He shook his head. "You don't make it easy. Not ever."

I sat down beside him in the gap of the oak. "I see that now. I didn't before." I wanted to reach for his hand, but the exasperation on his face stopped me. If I tried, he'd pull away, and then I'd lose my courage. "That's why I'm here. To say that I'm sorry." He stayed silent, and I pressed on, my hands shaking. "I know it wasn't you who took the Heartstring Pie recipe. I'm sorry I accused you of stealing it. I was wrong." He nodded, but when he still didn't say anything, my hopes flagged. "You're still mad?"

He blew out a heavy breath. "I'm mad because you thought I took it. But I'm even madder that you ever thought I would do something like that in the first place. You've always assumed the worst about me." He frowned. "After all this time, it's like you don't know me at all."

His words cut into me, making my skin burn. "You're right. I *did* assume the worst. I never understood it before, but I think I do now. All this time, through all of our stupid competitions, I . . . needed you. It may have seemed like you brought out the worst in me, but you pushed me to do better. And you called me on my flaws when no one else would. But the thing is . . ." I sucked in a breath, then let my next words pour out in a rush. ". . . it was always easier to get mad at you than it was to let myself . . . fall for you."

He lifted his head then, his eyes widening.

"You heard me right." I smiled through my nervousness. "Only . . . I know I might be too late. I saw Caroleen with you today, and if there's something—"

"There's not." His voice decisive. "Caroleen's not the one for me. Never will be." My heart lifted hopefully.

"She's not?" I whispered. "That's good, I mean . . . because the thing is . . ." I took a deep breath, then tried again. "I realize now that every time I got annoyed by you, it was really because of how much I actually liked you."

He stared out at the water, looking thoughtful. I waited as the minutes passed at a slug's pace, wondering what he was thinking but afraid to ask for fear of saying something that might destroy whatever precarious chances I had. When he faced me again, his eyes were open and hopeful.

"What about your temper?" he asked quietly.

I smiled sheepishly. "It's something I'm going to work on."

"Good!" He elbowed me. A slow smile tugged at the corners of his mouth, making him look completely adorable and even more completely kissable. As if he'd read my mind, he leaned toward me. "Bet I can out-kiss you," he whispered.

I smiled, my heart thrilling. "Bet you can't."

Our lips met with a soft warmth that stole my breath and made my head spin. My first kiss.

Suddenly, it was as if everything that was "supposed to be" about me and Chayton became truth. It had taken years of growing up for us to grow into each other, but here we were, together, at last. I never wanted our kiss to end, but a second later, a giant horse snout shoved its way between our heads, separating us.

"Flash!" Chayton and I said together, laughing.

I playfully pushed Flash's snout away.

"You're in high demand," Chayton teased, helping me to my feet.

"Funny," I said, smacking him lightly across the arm.

His eyes twinkled playfully. "Race you back to the stables?"

"Absolutely. But can I ask for a favor first? It has to do with the Heartstring Pie recipe. I need a couple days to do some research, but I think Zari and I might've found a way to keep the recipe safe."

"From my mom?" He raised an inquisitive eyebrow. "This I've got to hear."

Chapter Fourteen

I checked the strings on GG Hazel's apron, making sure they were double-knotted. The flower-patterned fabric was fraying slightly at the edges, but I loved wearing the apron. I felt at ease in it, and confident, as if I could conquer the world. I hadn't asked Mom for permission to take it down from its hallowed place beside GG Hazel's photo, but I guessed she wouldn't mind. Not for a special reason like this one.

Chayton glanced over at me and did a double take. "Whoa," he breathed. "You could be her twin."

Zari and Mr. Jenkins looked my way, and both of their jaws dropped.

"Who?" I asked. "Maybe this wasn't a good idea." I started to untie the apron. "I should take it off—"

"No!" all three of them said in unison.

Zari took me by the shoulders and turned me to face the photo on the wall. "Dace, look!"

I studied the photo, and my reflection in the new frame's glass, and gasped. In the apron, with my hair in its half updo, I really *was* the spitting image of GG Hazel.

"It's crazy how much you look like her," Zari said.

"So . . . this is a good thing?" I asked.

"Oh yeah. Viewers are going to eat that up." She went back to rummaging through her bag in search of lip gloss.

I shot Chayton a nervous glance, and he grinned. "It's a very good thing," he said. "Your GG Hazel was beautiful."

I blushed. "Thanks."

"Okay, I think we're ready," the newly lip-glossed Zari announced. "Should we do this?"

I took a deep breath. Since we'd come up with the idea two days ago, I'd spent every spare minute preparing for tonight.

Spare minutes didn't come easy, either. When I wasn't in school, I was running Pies N' Prattle along with the constantly rotating shifts of Bonneters who'd offered to help during Mom's recovery. Even though we'd canceled the pie-eating contest for Saturday's fair, there was still a lot to do. Mom had baked a handful of pies before her accident, but as it turned out, the only pie people really wanted was the Heartstring Pie, and that one was turning out to be my specialty. So I baked, and when our customers wanted a slice, they walked behind the counter to help themselves.

In a way, Mom's absence had worked to my advantage. It had given me the chance to talk to our customers about GG Hazel, to pick their brains for stories that I'd never heard before. I did some research at the Bonnet library and online, until finally I felt like I could talk about GG Hazel—not just as a legend, but as my great-grandma. As family.

That was what tonight was all about.

Mr. Jenkins took the tablet from Chayton.

"You sure you know how to work the video, Granddad?" Chayton asked for the tenth time.

Mr. Jenkins lifted a stern eyebrow in Chayton's direction. "Son, I can drive a herd of five hundred head of cattle. I can push a dang button."

"Just asking," Chayton said, holding up his hands to plead innocence. Then he joined me and Zari, the three of us forming a semicircle around GG Hazel's photo.

I nodded at Mr. Jenkins, who whispered, "Three. Two. One."

I smiled into the tablet's lens, trying not to think about how ridiculous my smile might look later on when we replayed this video. It didn't matter. I needed to do this. For Mom. And GG Hazel.

Beside me, Zari began talking to the camera. "Hey, y'all. This is Zari Trent, reporting for *The Beehive* in Bonnet, Texas. I'm bringing you a very special streaming edition of the Bonnet Buzz. It's special because Bonnet's very own Dacey Culpepper Biel, great-granddaughter of the renowned Hazel Culpepper, is going to bake Hazel's famous Heartstring Pie."

"I am." I beamed at the camera.

"And not only that!" Zari went on, "She's going to bake it with Chayton Freedell, son of *Prairie Living*'s Julip Freedell!"

Chayton waved to the camera. "Hey, everybody! Mom, if you're watching, please don't hate us for our stellar pie crusts!"

I had to hold back a laugh. I knew Chayton was taking a big risk agreeing to be in this video, and that Julip was probably going to be furious when she saw it. But Chayton was handling it in his typical laid-back fashion. "We're doing the right thing," he'd told me when I asked him if he was totally sure he wanted to go ahead with it. "And it's time I had a real talk with Mom anyway. Maybe this will jump-start the discussion."

"More like ignite it," I'd said, only half joking.

He'd taken my hand. "I'm okay with whatever happens. Really. I love my mom, but I need to be more honest with her about how hard things have been for me."

"So, Dacey," Zari said now, jolting me out of my thoughts. "Tell us about Hazel Culpepper and her Heartstring Pie. What's their story?"

This was it. What I said over the next few minutes might very well determine the fate of Pies N' Prattle, and GG Hazel's recipe. It was up to me. I straightened, acutely aware of GG Hazel's photo behind me, watching, waiting to see what I'd do.

"Well." I looked directly at the camera, unwavering. "The story of GG Hazel's Heartstring Pie really begins with a war and a candy bar. A Heath bar, to be exact." I smiled, feeling some of my nerves quiet. "During World War II, the US government distributed Heath candy bars to enlisted men who were fighting overseas. It gave the men a little taste of something sweet in the bitterest of times. And GG Hazel, she had a similar idea, but she wanted to capture that sweetness in a pie . . ."

I kept talking, forgetting all about the camera, or how many people might (or might not) watch the video once we uploaded it. GG Hazel's stories coursed through my veins, into my heart, and out of my mouth in a steady stream. There was the story Mrs. Beaumont had told me about her father, who'd come back from the war unable to speak. GG Hazel brought him Heartstring Pie every morning for three months straight, sitting with him through his quiet eating until, finally, one sunny morning, he said, "I don't suppose I could have a second slice of that pie?" There was the story of Mr. Walker's older brother in Dallas, who loved Hazel's pie so much that he drove a hundred miles every Sunday to eat a slice at Pies N' Prattle. And there were other stories, too. Dozens more.

I lost track of time as I talked, and probably would've kept going, if Zari hadn't touched my arm to bring my attention back to her.

"Dacey, you've got our mouths positively watering for a taste of this pie. Soooo . . . are you going to bake us some?" She smiled with the perfected poise of an interviewer, and I made a mental note to tell her later how awesome she was at this.

"Absolutely." I returned her smile. "But I'll need a little help, of course. Follow me." Mr. Jenkins followed us into the kitchen, where the ingredients for the Heartstring Pie were laid out on the counter. I turned to Chayton, adding teasingly, "Chayton Freedell, are you ready to bake the most famous pie in the entire state of Texas?"

Chayton feigned wiping sweat from his brow. "No pressure or anything, Dace." He grinned. "Will GG Hazel haunt me if I get it wrong?"

"*She* won't." I elbowed him. "But I might."

"That *is* a scary thought." He laughed as I tossed one of my oven mitts at him.

"Hooooh, things are heating up in this kitchen already!" Zari teased for the benefit of the camera. "So, what's the first step, Dacey?"

"It involves two of my favorite ingredients: chocolate chips and Heath bar." I lifted the bowls of chips and Heath chunks to the camera, and then began mixing ingredients alongside Chayton. We moved through the recipe's steps, starting with the cookies for the crust and then moving on to the pie filling. Chayton and I had fun the whole time, flicking spoonfuls of Heath bits and flour at each other and catapulting chocolate chips into each other's mouths.

"We've added in all the ingredients now," I said at last. "Except one."

"What ingredient is that?" Zari asked.

"The secret ingredient," I said. "One that we only have here, at Pies N' Prattle. Viewers can bake the pie as it is, without this ingredient. But only *our* Pies N' Prattle Heartstring Pie has GG Hazel's one-of-a-kind healing touch. It wasn't just the pie's ingredients that helped folks. It was GG Hazel herself. Her way of listening to people, or talking with them, laughing with them. I think she understood, in her own heart, what they needed to start healing. Her shop has always been a special place. I just wish I could promise that it will be around forever." My eyes suddenly misted over, and I fought to speak past the lump in my throat. "Only I can't. Business has been slow lately. Not just in our shop, but all around our town. And if that doesn't change, we don't know what will happen."

I swallowed, and continued. "So. If you want the real Heartstring Pie, the way GG Hazel made it, visit Bonnet and Pies N' Prattle while you still have the chance." My voice cracked on that last word, and I swiped at my eyes, trying hard not to give into my tears. Then, I took two handkerchiefs from a drawer. "And now, if you'll excuse me while I add in the last ingredient . . ."

I blindfolded Zari and Chayton like we'd decided to do beforehand, to heighten the suspense. Then, with Mr. Jenkins keeping the camera focused on Zari and Chayton in the kitchen, I carefully took the uncooked pie into the main room. The truth was that I didn't know if GG had ever added a secret ingredient to her version of Heartstring Pie, but this was going to be *my* secret ingredient from now on.

Holding the Heartstring Pie up to GG Hazel's picture, I whispered, "Let this help some hearts, GG. Today, tomorrow, and always."

I smiled at her photo, happiness sweeping over me. Then I walked back into the kitchen and slid the pie into the oven.

"And that's how you make Heartstring Pie," I announced as Chayton and Zari slipped off their blindfolds.

Mr. Jenkins hit PAUSE and lowered the tablet as Zari and Chayton whooped.

"That was amazing!" Zari said, giving me a high five.

Chayton hugged me. "You killed it."

"Thanks." I beamed. "So did you guys! Now all we have to do is the taste test when the pie's finished baking . . ."

"And then we upload the video to YouTube and see what happens," Zari said.

"Do you really think people are going to watch it?" I asked.

"I'll tell you what," Mr. Jenkins said. "People couldn't get enough of Heartstring Pie when your great-grandma was alive. It'll be the same this time, too. You wait and see."

"But what about Julip?" I asked worriedly. "The fair's the day after tomorrow, and she's already miffed that we had to cancel the pie-eating contest. Do you think she'll still go ahead with selling the Heartstring Pie recipe?"

"I don't see how she can," Mr. Jenkins said. "You're putting it out in the world on *your* terms. Anything she does now will be playing second fiddle to the great-granddaughter of GG Hazel baking Heartstring Pie."

I hoped with all my heart that he was right. "I guess we can clean up while we wait for the pie to finish baking—" My words died when I saw Chayton pulling out more bags of flour and sugar and dozens of aluminum pie pans from the cabinets. "Chayton? What are you doing?"

He gave me a look that said the answer should've been completely obvious. "Getting ready."

"For what?"

"For the hundreds of Heartstring Pies we're going to have to bake between now and Saturday."

I stared at him. "Chayton, we canceled the pie-eating contest. We don't need—"

"We will." He smiled at me. "Dace, nobody cares about the pie-eating contest. They care about the Heartstring Pie. And when they see your video, they're going to show up wanting a slice."

"I don't know," I began. "We'll use up most of the baking supplies, and . . ." My voice faltered. "It's a big risk with business as slow as it's been. Besides, how are we going to bake that many pies in less than forty-eight hours?"

Chayton held up his phone. "Already taken care of. I posted on the Bonnet Facebook page this morning, and over half the town responded. Everybody's going to work in shifts. And the first shift starts in . . ." He checked his watch. "Two hours. Right after we finish filming."

"But—but you posted before we filmed? How did you—"

"Hey, you're a Culpepper. Rumor has it that you're an unstoppable force. More than rumor, actually. I've witnessed it firsthand." He shrugged, giving me that grin that was so familiar and yet still made my knees weak. "All I did was keep the faith."

I threw my arms around him. "Thank you," I whispered, then blushed when I remembered that Mr. Jenkins was still standing there. Bashfully, I pulled away from Chayton, but when I glanced at Mr. Jenkins, he was looking on, smiling in approval.

"So?" Chayton handed me a stack of Heath bars.

I nodded. "Let's bake some pies."

Chapter Fifteen

I woke up long before my alarm on Saturday, roused by the sound of cars driving past our house. *Weird*, I thought. We never had traffic on Main Street, not even on fair day.

I showered and dressed in record time, adrenaline and exhaustion mixing to give me a heady excitement. I'd gone to bed at close to midnight after baking the three hundredth Heartstring Pie. The Pies N' Prattle ovens had been on for so long by then that the shop's kitchen felt like an inferno. We'd even started carrying the unbaked pies to people's houses to bake in *their* ovens. In the end, nearly every oven in Bonnet had baked a

Heartstring Pie and nearly every Bonneter—old and young—had helped mix pie filling or crush cookies for the crust.

Our video had been viewed nearly one hundred thousand times since we uploaded it on Thursday night. I knew that didn't mean that many people would show up to the fair, but it gave me a growing hope that maybe, just maybe, our plan would work.

I'd wanted to keep that plan a secret from my parents, but last night, Dad had shown up at the shop wearing his apron, and I knew the jig was up.

"How did you find out?" I asked.

Dad kissed the top of my head. "Honeybee, if you want to keep a conspiracy involving an entire town a secret, best not let your video air on the evening news."

"What?" I gaped at him.

He nodded. "On *all* the local news channels."

"Omigod. Does Mom know?" Mom had gotten the go-ahead from Doctor Higgins to attend the fair, but only if she stayed on brain rest until Saturday morning. She wasn't allowed to have any screen time, but that didn't mean she hadn't snuck her cell phone into her bedroom.

"Nope," Dad said. "There was no way I was going to spoil *this* surprise for her." And then he took up the measuring cups and set to work alongside Mrs. Beaumont and Mrs. Gonzalez.

Now, as I slipped on my shoes, I thought about how hard we had all worked over the last two days, and I made up my mind that, no matter what happened at the fair today, I wouldn't be disappointed. Even if all of the Heartstring Pies went uneaten, even if everything we'd done didn't help Pies N' Prattle or Bonnet, I was happy with knowing we'd done the best we could. GG Hazel, I thought, would've been happy knowing that, too.

When I walked into the kitchen, Dad was standing there wearing a grin as wide as the Rio Grande.

"Dad? Wha—"

"Shhhh," he whispered. He motioned toward the master bedroom, where I guessed Mom was still sleeping. "Come with me." He led me to the front door and opened it. I stared out at Main Street and gasped.

Last night, Julip's *Prairie Living* team had added finishing touches to Main Street for the fair, and in the bright light of morning, the heart of Bonnet looked beautiful. The shops and restaurants, which only weeks ago had looked worn and weary with their peeling paint and dark windows, now were blazing with vivid colors, streamers, and flower boxes. Paper lanterns and balloons were strung overheard, giving the street a carnival atmosphere.

None of that, though, was what made my jaw drop. The cars were what did.

Cars were parked headlight to taillight at every inch of curb. And there was a steady stream of cars—legitimate traffic!—driving in the direction of the Jenkins ranch, where the fairgrounds had been set up.

"Bonnet's first rush hour," Dad said. "Some of the license plates are from out of state! And they're all here for the fair."

"This is so amazing." A smile grew on my face. "But—" I checked myself. "They're probably just here for the chance to get on Julip's *Prairie Living* show."

"I thought that, too," Dad said, "until I took a little stroll over to the fairgrounds . . ."

My heart flipped. "What do you mean?"

He winked. "Why don't you walk on over and check it out? Oh, and you might want to bring GG Hazel's apron with you. Just saying."

My heart began racing. I didn't wait another second. I grabbed the apron from where I'd hung it on our coatrack the night before and took off at a run toward the Jenkins ranch.

The ranch was decorated just as impressively as Main Street, with festive balloon arches, brightly colored game booths, and carnival rides. And then there were food trucks, with their barbecue pits already smoking with ribs and cauldrons of chili and gumbo.

I wove past the mechanical bull, the pony rides, and the petting zoo, then came to a dead halt when I spotted the line of people. It snaked a long path through the booths and rides, arriving exactly where I hoped it would: at the Pies N' Prattle table.

Maria, Bree, and Zari were already standing behind the table, even though the fair wasn't scheduled to open for another two hours. They waved me over, but for a second, my feet wouldn't budge. It was too much to take in, that all these people could've driven from miles away just for a taste of Heartstring Pie.

I felt such a rush of deep relief and joy that I thought I might actually lift off the ground.

"Dacey?" a familiar voice said in my ear.

I turned to see Chayton smiling at me. "You okay?" he asked.

I nodded. "It's . . . I never expected this."

"I did. I expected nothing less of you. And it's not because you're a Culpepper. It's because you're *you*." There was a pride in his voice that made me blush, and I blushed even deeper when he slipped his arm around my waist. "Come on. You've got customers waiting. Technically, the fair's not open yet, but Granddad said he'd make an exception for you. Mostly because I don't think these people will do anything else until they've had a slice of your pie."

I laughed softly, but when I reached the table, the laugh was quashed by the sight of Julip and her camera crew hovering nearby. I gave Chayton a questioning glance, but he looked as surprised as I was.

"She wasn't here a minute ago," he whispered. "I swear."

I squeezed his hand. "It's okay."

I didn't hesitate or falter, but stepped right up to Julip, ready to face whatever curve balls she could throw my way.

"And here she is now!" Julip said as her crew swiveled the cameras to zoom in on my face. "The pride of Bonnet, and Hazel Culpepper's great-granddaughter, Dacey Culpepper Biel!" Julip leaned toward me, oozing friendly vibes. "Dacey, I for one am so proud to see that you've brought the Culpepper name back into the spotlight. Your video was absolutely charming! Thank you for bringing back Heartstring Pie."

I paused for a millisecond, just long enough for inspiration to strike me with the force of a lightning bolt. And then I was smiling bright for the cameras, perfectly at ease. "No, Ms. Freedell," I said evenly. "I'm the one who should be thanking you."

Julip blinked, and I knew I'd caught her off guard. "Oh? For what?"

"For taking such good care of our family's recipe. It's GG Hazel's original recipe, and I was so worried when it went missing, until I found out you had it." My smile spread. "Thank you for keeping it safe and sound for us." I held out my hand. "We're so grateful to be getting it back."

"Oh." The soft squeak in that *Oh* was the only thing that gave any hint of Julip's defeat. "Yes, well, it was an honor to hold it in my hands. A priceless family heirloom like that." She smiled seamlessly for the camera as she slid the piece of paper from her pocket into my palm. "Even for a little while."

I nodded. "I'd be glad to talk with you more about GG Hazel, but first, I think I have some pies to give out."

"Yes," Julip said dazedly. "Of course!" She motioned to the cameras. "Folks, let's head over to the food trucks to see if any of that delicious-smelling chili is ready for tasting!" She stepped away from me, and the cameras followed her.

I heaved a sigh of relief, and a second later, Maria, Bree, and Zari crushed me in a group hug.

"*That* was fantastic!" Maria whispered gleefully.

"Thank you so much, guys," I said. "What are you doing here early? I figured you'd be sleeping in." They'd baked for nearly as long as I had last night, and I knew how tired they were.

"You've got to be kidding." Zari waved at the line of customers. "I've got two hundred new subscribers to my Bonnet Buzz channel on YouTube. And I'll bet that somewhere in this line is someone who has connections at the *New York Times*. Six degrees of separation and all that." She pulled a stack of her *Beehive* business cards from her pocket. "Don't mind me. I'll be spending the next few hours networking."

She started for the line, but I called after her teasingly, "Wait a sec. Aren't you going to help me hand out pie?"

"Well, there's a little bit of a problem with that," Bree said.

Maria nodded. "Most of these people want to talk to *you*."

I balked. "What? Come on . . ." But my disbelieving laugh died in my throat when I glanced at the first woman in line—a frail, weathered woman who looked like she might've been close to one hundred. Her ancient eyes were gazing at me expectantly.

"Excuse me, young lady." Her voice trembled. "Are you Hazel Culpepper's great-granddaughter?"

I nodded, and she reached out an impossibly slender hand, her eyes filling. "I knew your GG Hazel. She gave me a slice of her pie once." She smiled. "And I've been waiting all these years for a second slice."

"I'd love to hear that story." My heart swelled as I cut a generous piece of Heartstring Pie and handed it to her. She took her first bite, her eyes lit up, and she began talking. And that was the beginning of the stories. With each slice and each new customer came a different story. Some of the stories were happy; some were sad, but they all seemed to have one thing in common: They all needed to be shared with me.

It took a couple of stumbling starts, but after the first few customers, I figured out what my real job was. It wasn't to hand out slices of pie. Zari, Maria, Bree, Chayton—they could all help with that. My job was to listen, and even, when needed, take someone's hand or offer them a hug.

It felt even more natural than baking the Heartstring Pie had.

Finally, when the sun had climbed to an impressive height in the cloudless sky, I glanced up to see that the last person in line was my mom.

She smiled at me, a few stray tears spilling down her cheeks. "I'm speechless, Dace," she choked out, and grabbed me in a fierce hug.

"You? Speechless?" I murmured into her shoulder. "Never."

Mom laughed. "I know. You're right. That would be impossible." She stood back to look at me. "I've been watching you for the last hour, and I'm so proud. So very proud. What you've done." She waved her hand at the nearly empty pie table. "Well. It's incredible. And do you know that Julip actually apologized to me?"

I gaped. "Really?"

Mom nodded. "Came up to me and admitted to taking the recipe, and even started crying. I think she really has had a rough time lately with the show. It's too bad, and I wanted to make her feel better . . ."

"Mom? You didn't actually—"

"Of *course* I offered her a slice of Heartstring Pie! I had to!"

I laughed. "You're unstoppable."

"So are you. *And* you're a natural. You're going to take my place someday—"

"Mom," I stopped her. "I'm not going to take anybody's place. I want to take my own."

Mom smiled. "Yes. Exactly."

"But . . . those hundreds of Heartstring Pies." I met her eyes. "Mom, I *gave* them all away. How did that help Pies N' Prattle?"

"Dacey, let me show you something." Mom took out her phone and pulled up email. "Five hundred emails to my Pies N' Prattle account since Thursday. They're all from potential customers wanting to place orders for pies. Not Heartstring Pie, but every other pie we make. And they're from all over the country." She grinned. "Dace, we're going to have to start selling pies nation-wide. Shipping them out of state. I didn't want to do that before, but now . . . why not? Heartstring Pie will only be available *at* the shop. But our other pies? Why not let everyone enjoy them, no matter where they live?"

"Wow," I breathed, scarcely able to believe it. "But what about the other businesses in Bonnet? The Gonzalezes and everyone else?"

"I don't know," Mom said, "but I'm hopeful. We all are." She hugged me again. "You've given us that."

I glanced around. The fair was in full swing now, and I saw that Mom was right. Ms. Jackson sat with her laptop on a picnic blanket, happily typing and nibbling Heartstring Pie. Doctor and Mrs. Higgins were sharing a slice as they rode the Ferris wheel. Little Alma was eating a slice as she sat on Mrs. Gonzalez's lap, listening to Julip conduct an interview with Mr. Gonzalez about The Whole Enchilada while Marco gurgled happily. Everywhere I looked were Bonneters laughing, smiling, hugging, enjoying the moment. It was as if the town had been sitting under a gray cloud for so long, but now the sun was shining bright and full.

Then I saw Chayton walking toward me. Mom followed my gaze, then elbowed me. "That's my cue. I'm off to find your dad. That man always rides the Tilt-A-Whirl one too many times . . ."

She blew me a kiss as she left, and then Chayton was beside me, holding a pie box in his hands. My heart performed the little happy dance it always did when I was near him.

"Hey, are you okay?" I asked. "You disappeared when I was talking to your mom before and I thought maybe—"

"That I was mad?" A trace of sadness flickered across his face. "I was. But not at you." He paused. "It's more like I'm disappointed. Sometimes I have a hard time dealing with the fact that my mom's probably not ever going to change."

"I'm sorry." I held his gaze.

"Me too," he said. "*But* . . . I don't want to spend today being sorry. Because today is *your* day. And anyway, I have some good news. At least, *I* think it's good news."

"*More* good news?" I laughed. "How could there possibly be more?"

He grinned. "What if I told you that when my mom leaves for her next filming location, I'm staying here instead of going with her?"

"Really?"

He nodded. "Granddad and Granny want me to stay with them. I love working on the ranch, and Mom travels so much . . . This was a good solution. I'll still see Mom every week or so when she comes back to Bonnet between filming, and I can travel with her whenever I want to. This just works out better for everybody right now."

"That *is* good news." I smiled at him, loving the way his eyes lit up at my words. "That means we'll have so much more time for spelling bee competitions, and pie-throwing matches, and—"

"Pie-baking contests?" he finished, nodding to the pie box in his hands.

"No." I stared in disbelief. "You didn't."

"Oh, I did. I made it just for you. I call it Head Over Heels pie." Chayton opened the lid to reveal a pie plate piled high with gummy hearts, heart-shaped lollipops, and chocolate hearts.

I burst out laughing. "*That* is the ugliest pie I've ever seen."

"*But . . .*" He grinned. "It was made by the sweetest guy you've ever seen."

I laughed again—and then I noticed the words written clumsily in white icing over the top of the candies. *My heartstring is forever tied to yours.* My pulse cartwheeled as I looked up at Chayton. "That was what was written under the stool at the Bonnet soda shop."

He nodded. "I wrote that. On the pie and . . ." He sucked in a breath. "Under the seat at the shop. The day after we tied for the fourth-grade spelling bee." He blushed burgundy. "You always sat in that seat, and well, I wrote the words for you. Back then . . . and now."

"Chayton." My heart burst into a thousand fireflies of happiness. "I had no idea . . ."

"It's always been you, Dace," he whispered. "I thought maybe if I wrote the words, somehow you'd know in your heart, and you'd fall head over heels for me."

I glanced down again at the words on the pie. "Head Over Heels pie. It *does* have a nice ring to it."

Chayton grinned, looking immensely relieved that he'd exposed his heart to me, and I hadn't trampled it, and that we could still tease each other. Teasing and having fun was what we seemed best at. "I thought so," he said, playing along.

"And I suppose you want me to taste it to see what happens?"

"Only if you're willing to risk the consequences."

I cocked an eyebrow at him, then reached into the pie box and plucked out a chocolate heart. I bit into it, then fake-swooned, making him drop the pie box and catch me in his arms.

"Did it work?" he whispered in my ear.

A thrill shot through me as I looked into his eyes. "Not yet. It's missing something. A special ingredient." I leaned close and gave him a sweet kiss. He wrapped his arms around me and kissed me back. Then I smiled up at him. "Yep. Head over Heels is definitely my favorite kind of pie."

Pies N' Prattle Recipes

Are you ready for the cozy comfort of a slice of
Pies N' Prattle magic? Give some of these recipes
a try, and you'll fall head over heels for their
sweetness! Just remember to always have adult
supervision when you're using an oven or
stovetop, or handling hot foods.

Dacey's Berry Chocolate Pie

Ingredients for pie crust:
- Parchment or wax paper
- 2 store-bought pie crusts
- 3 Tbsp unsweetened baking cocoa powder
- 1 Tbsp powdered sugar

Directions for pie crust:

Unroll each individual pie crust onto a counter covered with parchment or wax paper. Scoop 1½ tablespoons of cocoa powder and ½ tablespoon of powdered sugar into the middle of each circle of dough. Fold the edges of the crust toward the middle and start kneading. Knead the dough for several minutes, until the color becomes a uniform brown and the sugar and cocoa are thoroughly blended into the dough. Once you have two balls of dough, roll each back out with a rolling pin. Put aside until ready to use.

Ingredients for pie filling:
- 1 cup fresh blueberries
- 1 cup fresh blackberries
- 1 cup fresh raspberries
- 1 cup quartered strawberries
- ½ cup granulated white sugar
- ¼ cup minute tapioca
- 1 Tbsp vanilla extract
- 1½ cups semisweet chocolate morsels

Directions for pie filling and baking:

Preheat oven to 350° Fahrenheit. Wash and dry all of the berries and place in a large mixing bowl. Add ½ cup sugar and ¼ cup tapioca to the berries. Stir gently until combined and let sit for fifteen minutes so tapioca can soften and absorb the berry juice. Pour in 1 tablespoon vanilla extract and ½ cup semisweet chocolate morsels and stir.

Press one pie crust into the bottom of an ungreased glass pie pan. Pour 1 cup semisweet chocolate morsels into the bottom of the pan and spread them into an even layer. Pour the berry and chocolate pie filling over the layer of chocolate morsels. Cover the pie filling with the second pie crust and crimp the edges of the dough. Place thin strips of aluminum foil around the outside of the pie pan to keep the upper crust's edges from burning. Using a knife, make several small slits in the top of the crust.

Place the pie in the oven and bake for approximately 50–60 minutes, or until the crust is cooked thoroughly and the filling is bubbly. Enjoy!

Chayton's Caramel Apple Pie

Ingredients for homemade pie crust:
    Parchment paper
    2 cups flour
    1 Tbsp powdered sugar
    1 Tsp salt
    ¾ cup cold unsalted butter, cubed
    ⅓–½ cup buttermilk (add more as needed)

Directions for homemade pie crust:
    Combine flour, sugar, and salt in a standing mixer. Add the cubed
    butter until the dough forms pea-sized lumps. Pour ⅓ cup butter-
    milk into the mixer and blend. The dough should still be crumbly
    but should be sticky enough to mold into larger pieces by hand.
    Turn off the mixer and, using your hands, press and shape the
    dough into one large ball. Then, divide the ball in half and shape
    again into two separate balls. Wrap these in plastic wrap and
    refrigerate for at least an hour, or freeze for 15–20 minutes.
    Remove the chilled dough from the refrigerator or freezer, and
    using a rolling pin, roll out the dough onto a sheet of parchment
    or wax paper until you have two flat, circular crusts. Set aside.

Alternative directions for super-easy pie crusts:
    Two store-bought pie crusts, and *voilà*, you're done! ☺

For pie filling:
    5–6 cored, peeled, and sliced Granny Smith apples
    ½ cup granulated white sugar
    1 Tsp cinnamon
    Caramel sauce

For caramel sauce:
- ½ cup white granulated sugar
- ⅓ cup water
- 2 Tbsp butter
- ¾ cup heavy cream
- ½ Tbsp vanilla extract

Directions for pie filling and baking:

Preheat oven to 425° Fahrenheit. Wash and dry 5-6 peeled, cored, and sliced Granny Smith apples. Place them in a large mixing bowl. Add ½ cup sugar and 1 teaspoon cinnamon to the apples and stir until combined. Prepare the caramel sauce in a medium saucepan on the stovetop. Pour ½ cup sugar into the saucepan and make level. Add ⅓ cup water and stir over medium heat until the sugar is dissolved and the liquid becomes clear. Turn up the heat to medium high and stir until the sugar mixture caramelizes, turning a golden brown. Add 2 table-spoons butter, stirring until melted. Remove from heat and add ¾ cup heavy cream and ½ tablespoon of vanilla extract. Stir all ingredients until the caramel mixture is syrupy in texture. Set aside.

Press one pie crust into the bottom of an ungreased glass pie pan. Pour the caramel sauce into the bottom of the pan. Pour the apple filling over the caramel sauce. Cover the pie filling with the second pie crust and crimp the edges of the dough. Place thin strips of aluminum foil around the outside of the pie pan to keep the crust's edges from burning. Using a knife, make several small slits in the top of the crust.

Place the pie in the oven and bake for approximately 50-60 minutes, or until the crust is golden brown and the filling is bubbly. Enjoy!

GG Hazel's Famous Heartstring Pie

For pie crust:
  Parchment paper
  1 tube store-bought premixed chocolate chip cookie dough (or
  you can make a batch of homemade chocolate chip cookie dough!
  Whatever you prefer!)
  ½ cup Heath Toffee Bits (found in the aisle alongside baking
  chocolate morsels at your grocery store)

Directions for pie crust:
  Spray the bottom and sides of a glass pie pan with cooking spray. Cut a circle of parchment paper to fit the bottom
  of the pie pan and place the paper in the bottom of the pan.
  Combine the raw cookie dough with ½ cup Heath Toffee Bits,
  stirring until well blended. Press the raw dough into the bottom
  and sides of pan to form a thin layer, which will bake into
  a crust. Set the pan aside. (Note: If you'd prefer to use a cookie
  crumb crust, crush 12-14 store-bought or homemade chocolate chip cookies and combine with 1½ tablespoons melted
  butter. Don't forget to add the Heath Toffee Bits. Stir until
  the crumbs stick lightly together. Press into the bottom of the
  pie pan.)

For pie filling:
  ½ cup butter, softened
  1½ cups white granulated sugar
  3½ Tbsp flour
  1 Tbsp vanilla

3 large eggs
¾ cup buttermilk
½ cup semisweet chocolate morsels
¾ cup Heath Toffee Bits
Insert your own secret ingredient here!

Directions for pie filling and baking:

Preheat oven to 350° Fahrenheit. In a large mixing bowl and a hand mixer, combine the softened butter, sugar, flour, vanilla, and eggs. Blend on medium speed for approximately two minutes. Pour in ¾ cup buttermilk and blend for an additional minute. Spoon in ½ cup semisweet chocolate morsels and ¾ cup Heath Toffee Bits. Stir until combined. Add your special secret ingredient and stir. Pour the mixture into the pie pan.

Wrap aluminum foil around the bottom of the glass pie pan. (This will prevent the cookie dough crust from burning.) Bake the pie for approximately 60–65 minutes, until the middle of the pie is set (it will be slightly jiggly). Don't worry if the top of the pie turns dark brown. This is normal and means you've created a natural, deliciously buttery top crust! If it looks like it's beginning to burn, you can cover it loosely with aluminum foil for the last 10–15 minutes of baking. Let the pie cool at least 30–45 minutes before eating, because the filling will get firmer as it cools. Enjoy, and remember: One heart today, GG Hazel, and more hearts tomorrow!

About the Author

Suzanne Nelson has written several children's books, including *Cake Pop Crush*, *You're Bacon Me Crazy*, *Macarons at Midnight*, *Hot Cocoa Hearts*, *Donut Go Breaking My Heart*, and *Sundae My Prince Will Come*. She lives with her family in Ridgefield, Connecticut, where she can also be found experimenting with all kinds of cooking. Learn more about Suzanne at suzannenelson.com, or follow her on Twitter at @snelsonbooks or on Instagram at @suzannenelsonbooks.

Don't miss these
delicious reads
by Suzanne Nelson!

Find more reads you will love . . .

Vanesa Campos can't wait for winter vacation. Her week at Pinecloud Lodge promises skiing, hot cocoa, and maybe even some new friends. But suddenly, Vanesa's little brother, Hunter, is stranded out in the blizzard! Vanesa will have to team up with snooty Beck and twins Emma and Eric—plus one giant dog—to rescue him. Can she save her brother and discover which real friends will weather the storm with her?

Have you read all the Wish books?

- [ ] *Clementine for Christmas* by Daphne Benedis-Grab
- [ ] *Carols and Crushes* by Natalie Blitt
- [ ] *Allie, First at Last* by Angela Cervantes
- [ ] *Gaby, Lost and Found* by Angela Cervantes
- [ ] *Sit, Stay, Love* by J. J. Howard
- [ ] *Pugs and Kisses* by J. J. Howard
- [ ] *The Boy Project* by Kami Kinard
- [ ] *Best Friend Next Door* by Carolyn Mackler
- [ ] *11 Birthdays* by Wendy Mass
- [ ] *Finally* by Wendy Mass
- [ ] *13 Gifts* by Wendy Mass
- [ ] *The Last Present* by Wendy Mass
- [ ] *Graceful* by Wendy Mass
- [ ] *Twice Upon a Time: Beauty and the Beast, the Only One Who Didn't Run Away* by Wendy Mass
- [ ] *Twice Upon a Time: Rapunzel, the One with All the Hair* by Wendy Mass
- [ ] *Twice Upon a Time: Sleeping Beauty, the One Who Took a Really Long Nap* by Wendy Mass

- [ ] *Blizzard Besties* by Yamile Saied Méndez

- [ ] *Playing Cupid* by Jenny Meyerhoff

- [ ] *Cake Pop Crush* by Suzanne Nelson

- [ ] *Macarons at Midnight* by Suzanne Nelson

- [ ] *Hot Cocoa Hearts* by Suzanne Nelson

- [ ] *You're Bacon Me Crazy* by Suzanne Nelson

- [ ] *Donut Go Breaking My Heart* by Suzanne Nelson

- [ ] *Sundae My Prince Will Come* by Suzanne Nelson

- [ ] *I Only Have Pies for You* by Suzanne Nelson

- [ ] *Confectionately Yours: Save the Cupcake!* by Lisa Papademetriou

- [ ] *My Secret Guide to Paris* by Lisa Schroeder

- [ ] *Sealed with a Secret* by Lisa Schroeder

- [ ] *Switched at Birthday* by Natalie Standiford

- [ ] *The Only Girl in School* by Natalie Standiford

- [ ] *Once Upon a Cruise* by Anna Staniszewski

- [ ] *Deep Down Popular* by Phoebe Stone

- [ ] *Revenge of the Flower Girls* by Jennifer Ziegler

- [ ] *Revenge of the Angels* by Jennifer Ziegler